EMILY SHORE

THE TEMPLE
Copyright ©2019 Emily Shore
All rights reserved.
Printed in the United States of America
First Edition: November 2019

www.CleanTeenPublishing.com

SUMMARY: Trapped by Force, Serenity is required to become Yang—the bearer of her father's dark Temple legacy. Her new persona requires using a whip on her shell of a twin sister, but Serenity has even bigger problems. Most chillingly, a series of corpses with swan symbols carved in their chests. More than ever, Serenity needs Sky... and he will be there to protect her. No matter what it takes.

ISBN: 978-1-63422-366-9 (paperback)
ISBN: 978-1-63422-365-2 (e-book)
Cover Design by: Marya Heidel
Typography by: Courtney Knight
Editing by: Cynthia Shepp

PHOTO CREDITS:
© ornitozavr/fotolia
© nespix/fotolia
© matusciac/fotolia
© yuriyzhuravov/fotolia
© matusciac/fotolia

Young Adult Fiction / Dystopian
Young Adult Fiction / Social Themes / Sexual Abuse
Young Adult Fiction / Social Themes / Self-Esteem & Self-Reliance
Young Adult Fiction / Fantasy / Dark Fantasy

For more information about our content disclosure, please utilize the QR code above with your smart phone or visit us at www.CleanTeenPublishing.com

For Walter of Walter's Flying Bus who inspired Sunshine

PART One

One

HeRMoTher's DaugHter

BLISS

MY LAST CLIENT FOR THE night injects himself into me, teeth grazing my neck. He sweats his heart onto my skin, but it doesn't penetrate. Many whisper sweet nothings in my ear. Words like 'I love you,' 'stay with me,' and 'I'll want you forever,' are always sweet nothings. No better than snowflakes on the tongue. Tasteless and cold.

I think of my mother.

When I was a child, I dreamed my mother would come back for me. My father ground those dreams to dust long ago. Because I am not the special twin. I am the weak one who needed blood transfusions and oxygen to survive.

My father has never wanted me to see a photograph of my mother, but I've always known how close he keeps them. He has countless sprite lights in his master bedroom, including mine. One simple tap to bring them to life, but she's the only one he doesn't keep in his database. Hers are the only printed photos tucked away in an old book under his bed.

Tonight, he's sleeping deep, so I tiptoe into his room. All the training he established in my life from an early age gives me the ability to wander in and out—silent as a mouse's ghost.

It's difficult to see him sleeping. Even in dreams, I imagine he is still building onto his sky-city, not satisfied until the scraper stabs the stars and sucks the light out of them, too.

I steal the book, then scurry to my room to trace the photographs.

She is beautiful. I am just an eerie reflection of her—Father's silent Temple pawn, who rarely ever gets a lull from clients. Only in these barest moments before dawn.

Caught halfway between fawn and doe, my mother passed her gray eyes to me. Her apple cheeks, soft doll skin, and the slender curve of her neck, too. Even her curves are mine. Unicorn curves, my father says—the fable kind men will spend their lives searching for. He's usurped all to his advantage. From corporate moguls and royal dignitaries, infamous graphickers and foreign ambassadors, thriving oil barons and old wealth cultural elites... not one powerful station has missed my curves. They all have their different flavors and preferences. Different instructions and tastes. At the end of the day, they are all the same.

I keep them close, holding a thousand bits and pieces of skin, bones, muscles, sweat, sinew, tongues, stubble, and cologne—all of which I've used to erect a mountain around my heart. No love to feel.

When my mother left my father, she shattered his heart. An uncut diamond shredding that vital organ.

Nothing but scraps for me.

All this time, all these years, he's never given up his search for her. Or the baby she took. My sister.

I press down on my wrist tattoo with embedded computer that wills the volumetric projection just above my hand. Returning to a previous entry, I scan the footage of my sister and her last Swan dive exhibit. I watch her body, so like our mother's and mine, but she moves differently. She moves like Father. Too much spirit. Too much mania. When the director's body tangles with hers, I flick the screen off, disinterested in how he crushed his mouth to hers. Her resistance, too, even if it's the first time in Museum history a director became part of an exhibit.

She's special to Father. Why shouldn't she be special to the rest of the world? He says her name is Trinity.

I should not fault her as much as our mother, but I want to. The knowledge of our time in the womb, our first breaths ended with her free but me left in the hospital for the first month, clinging desperately to life...I try to convince myself it's not her fault, but when I look into her Swan eyes and see how different they are,

I believe she must have sucked me dry. Like our father, she fought harder. Like our mother, she escaped and left nothing but the scraps. Scraps that are never enough for Father. Scraps he's used again and again, hoping to find some purpose, but I know the truth. He will never have purpose until he finds her again. Until he finds them both.

"Mara."

I startle at his voice. My new name—a *bitter* reminder of what he lost. When I look up with a frail expression because he's caught me with the book, I expect him to ask me to go into his closet for the whip. Instead, he cups my cheek, staring down at me with a smile. My automatic assumption is a singular client. Father doesn't give me much of a reprieve between them, so healing through the Implant isn't an option.

"She is mine, Mara." He strokes my dark hair, and I wait in silence because it's what he expects, what he wants. "Your mother is mine again. And it won't be long before we have your sister inside these walls where she belongs. Serafina has changed much over the years. It's the first time I haven't managed to get her to speak, but I think it is time for you to meet her."

He extends a hand to raise me from the floor, sweeps the hair from my neck, but I don't tremble once. I stopped shuddering years ago at my father's close touch.

"Come with me. I will introduce you."

It's the first time I've wanted to tremble. Show some emotion. It's only natural for a girl meeting her mother for the first time—a mother who gave no thought or consideration before scooping up her golden child and leaving the broken one behind. To my father, I will be nothing more than a broken doll. Even if I've spent all these years building myself up again and again.

My father opens the door to his Breakable Room. It's an urban legend this room gave birth to the same name handed down to girls in the Glass District. The broken glass décor of the floor returns memories in waves. Although the walls are all glass, it's always reminded me of a padded room with no possibility to see the outside world.

Force guides me inside where I see my mother for the first time. She's a figurine from a music box. A paper doll I once played with as a child. Smaller than I thought. With how crumpled she is, I imagine I could fit her into the palm of my hand. Her clothes dangle off her skin, fitting more like loose rags because that is my father's preference. His orphan girl fantasy. One of many playing in his head like wind-up ballerina dolls. Her eyes look sick. The Breakable Room will do that.

Then, she faces me. Suddenly, her gray eyes become cathedral doors. She unfolds herself, rising from the corner she's since painted herself into. I stand still. Keep my eyes as iron shells. I can't break because there is nothing left unbroken. However, her piteous hand reaches out for me, sleeve dipping down one shoulder in response. There, I can see the hint of her past—a *memory* of a scar. No fresh ones. My father is biding his time.

"Bliss…"

It's the first time anyone has said my name that way. It's always been whispered as nothing-lust in my ear. She says it differently. Like there are no hidden agendas or motivations.

I don't move when she touches me. Her fingers light on my cheek, softer than a leaf dropping on a pond's surface. What I want is to deny it, to acknowledge this is simply one of Father's party tricks. After all, he's never imparted a gift without strings attached, but the next words out of her mouth confirm this visit has nothing to do with me. It's a means to an end.

"Why?" she asks my father, voice hoarse and withered.

Placing his hands behind his back, he circles her. "I thought I might try honey with you instead, Serafina. Vinegar wasn't working. That will change once I possess what is rightfully mine. For now, she is beyond my reach. But I will allow you one visit per day with Mara. All I want is her name. Her *real* name," he specifies while circlipng to stand in front of her again, blocking my body from hers.

I step to the side, and my mother stares at me before sinking her head, pursing her lips together, and succumbing. "Serenity. Her name is Serenity."

Two

BargAins

SERENITY

KY PEELS AWAY THE LAST of the prosthetics from my skin just as the sun sucks the leftover starry glitter in the sky outside our glass prison. If he hadn't been here to help me through the past couple of weeks, I'd have gone insane.

"Your father will be coming today," Sky notes, frustration creasing his forehead.

I nod.

My father has made a routine of checking on me at least once a day. We eat our breakfasts together. Well…not the first breakfast. That ended up on the floor, but I couldn't continue to justify wasting food. Especially not Temple food.

Force has resented my faux face as much as I have. He never knocks. At least the suite is spacious with a lower-level sitting area, so if I'm in the upper bedroom, I can hear the click of the door opening to give me enough warning.

"You have no idea how many times I've just wanted to climb down from one of these rafters and stab him in the jugular."

"The feeling is mutual." I grimace. "But we need to find out more. For all we know, he could have my parents in a holding center separate from the Penthouse." My half-hearted response doesn't convince Sky. He knows my real motivation. I can't risk losing him, too.

"He hasn't been very forthcoming during his time with you. What makes you think anything will change today?"

I gesture to my real face. "Because I'm finally me again."

5

Coiling one hand around my neck, he tilts his forehead to mine. "Yes. If there's anything good about this day, it's I can finally kiss you like I should. Your old mouth didn't quite fit mine like it's supposed to."

Sky doesn't hold back. For the first time in weeks, from keeping me warm to holding me through my rage and tears—yet never once stepping over the boundaries we've set—Sky doesn't hold back.

He doesn't smell the same. Too much time in the Temple. Clothes more metallic from the rafters, exploring every nook and cranny of the Temple's behind-the-scenes world. By now, I'm certain Sky's memorized every back route of the Penthouse. One Sanctuary-tech item he brought with him was a camo-device to help him blend in to any environment as well as tricking motion or heat sensors. Thanks to my father's generosity in allowing me to order whatever I want from the food printer, I've seen to it Sky never goes hungry. My only fear is we will both become part of this place. Like one of the many twisted glass pieces my father chooses to decorate his empire.

Thanks to the Immortal implant in my skin, Sky can't get me out. My father always wears my location embedded in the Temple system within his brain because, of course, my father would have a brain interface. The entire Temple bows to him. Except for Sky, whose cloaking device keeps him under the radar.

For now, we must hold onto our lightning and thunder to fuel the fire in our hearts for Force. He doesn't deserve the title of father.

I pull away before Sky can sink farther into my mouth. Closing my eyes, I turn around and rub my face, groaning because I can't even manage to accept a kiss without thoughts of that monster creeping into my head.

"What?" Sky wants to know. He doesn't pressure me. Only winds his arms around my waist, chin nuzzling my shoulder.

"It's just—this place. It's my father and the Temple. Up till now, we haven't even talked about us because of my face—"

Sky cuts me off, hands on my waist urging me to turn. "You think that's the only reason?" Rolling his eyes, he cups my cheeks. "Oh, Serenity. You will always be my silly, insufferable, beautiful girl. Yes, I love your face. I love every speck of your skin, marrow, bones, and heart—butterflies included."

I smirk at the analogy I adopted long ago for the inner workings of my fickle heart. The one I revealed the first night we spent in the Temple.

"But your soul matters most to me. And I won't jeopardize that soul." His eyes shift from side to side, reflecting. "You're only seventeen. And I'm twenty-one."

I narrow my brows, a little stunned. "You're talking about things like age and virtue? Here in the Temple? Really?"

"Because Kerrick and your mother raised us to know better. They might not have had the chance. But we do."

"But in this world, what's the point?" I wonder if he can sense the hesitation in my voice, my words more of a test than anything. Despite having lost all my dignity, the little I have left, I would never want to lose it in the Temple.

Sky's hands warm my cheeks to a flush when he says, "Because we can beat this world. Together."

I PASS THE MOMENTS UNTIL my father comes by exploring the fish inside the enormous fish tank. Cylindrical shaped, at least twenty feet wide, its foundation is rooted in the suite's lower level and continues in a spiral all the way up to the bedroom ceiling. Koi fish flit around inside. This suite was specially designed for my *watery* love. At night, I'll even indulge in the virtual landscape above my bed. All I need to do is press the button and my ceiling transforms into an underwater world complete with fish, stingrays, dolphins, whales, and even a shark or two. I don't want the swans.

The bedroom also features glass floor-to-ceiling windows for an uninhibited view of the Boroughs...and the country. Two more singular characteristics I can't ignore in this suite: the dining room chandelier—glowing, frosted, and swan-shaped—and the crystal Skeleton Flowers arranged in flowing patterns along the walls.

As soon as I hear the door's click from below, I stand straight, eyes venomous, hands still on the balcony just outside my bedroom that overlooks the brief hall to the sitting area where my father appears.

"Good to have my daughter back again," he addresses me, casual hands behind his back while pacing the lower level.

At first, I wonder why he doesn't invade the upstairs as he normally does, but I just cross my arms with a huff. "You could have had the prosthetics removed when I first got here," I remind him, disgust lathering my words.

"And miss out on the opportunity to discipline you? Tsk, tsk, tsk…"

Ignoring him, I jut out my chin. "Where's my mother?"

"You ask the same question every day. Care to try something more interesting?"

He doesn't sound irritated by my repetitive inquiry. No, he's far too pleased with himself.

"Substance over style," I counter.

My father drops his arms to his sides for one moment before raising his index finger to the air. "I shouldn't be surprised at your persistence. You are *my* daughter after all."

"There's no need to get insulting," I spit out.

Still casual, my father wanders toward the staircase and extends a hand. "Let us enjoy our first real meal together. Shall we?"

As I slide my hand down the banister, I keep my words just as light and airy, playing along. "Eating one of your glass sculptures would be more enjoyable, but if you insist…"

My father chuckles as I finish descending until I'm close enough for him to touch my hand. There is nothing gentle in the way he tugs me down to his level. Nothing gentle in the way the corners of his mouth spread into a smile like a proud flag unfolding itself. Nothing gentle when he plants that mouth on my forehead, lingering longer than I prefer because he's breathing in my scent.

"You will enjoy yourself this morning," my father assures me while cupping my chin. "You see, I've arranged for a couple of visitors to join us. They've been quite concerned about your welfare."

I shouldn't be surprised to see the bedroom doors open with no one near them since Force controls everything. Another moment passes before two men step into the doorway, and I jerk myself from Force and sprint for them. Or rather—one of them. The only one with no hidden agendas—even if he is a flirty jackass.

I hurl myself right into Neil's arms.

"Nice to see you too, beautiful," Neil comments, embracing me. "You're gonna make me blush." That's Neil. What I see is what I get. Not to mention how much I've missed his humor.

I thread my arms around his neck before hugging him again. "He figured it out before I could—"

"You don't have to apologize." He shrugs. "Was my idea. No good looking back at it."

"It was a clever one, son," Force commends him, approaching and offering Neil a backhanded compliment. "Your mistake was assuming I wouldn't know my own daughter."

Neil's hands linger on my elbows before he tugs my arms down and gestures to Luc, whose spine is like the back of a needle.

I nod to him. "Luc."

"Serenity."

My fingers play with each other, unsure of what else to do. Our last interaction wasn't exactly the greatest to say the least. Luc can't get under my skin like he used to anymore. After he tried to take the only thing I had left to my name to keep me from going to the Temple, all the ice he'd planted in my heart melted. Now, there's just Sky's warmth. Our lightning and thunder united with a drive more earth-shattering than ever before—to take down Force.

"No telling where your other admirer is," my father says, referring to Sky while popping open a bottle of champagne sitting on a nearby table and pouring glasses for all of us. "After all, judging by how he seemed that day at Luc's house, I'm surprised by how remarkably difficult he is to locate. Perhaps he's plotting your impossible escape."

He approaches me with a glass, foam bubbling up to the lip. He offers two more glasses to the men on my right. Neil raises his eyebrows, but accepts and downs his in one flamboyant gesture. Luc thumbs the side of his glass, contemplative. I'm a little more dramatic.

"Serenity," my father scolds just after I've chucked the glass, spilling the champagne and shattering the glass. The spill reminds me of a tiny silver creek with miniature crystals inside.

"You're missing out," Neil remarks while grabbing the rim of the bottle and pointing to it. "Ten-thousand-dollar bottle." Tipping it into his mouth, he gulps back a fair amount.

"Make yourself at home, Neil. It's what you do best." The loathing my father feels for his son is not lost on me.

"Why don't we all sit, enjoy our meal, and discuss some things?" Force invites us all to the table.

Luc tightens his other hand into a fist. "Give me one good reason why I shouldn't strangle you and drag Serenity out of this cage?"

My father smirks, clearly unconcerned while pulling out my chair. "Come now, Luc. We are both directors. Surely we can find some suitable arrangement."

I follow my father. "How about your head on a platter?" I opt while sliding into the chair.

Force plays with the ends of my hair, then leans over to murmur in my ear. "Trust me, daughter. My head on a platter is nowhere near in your best interests."

"Oh?" I play along. "And why is that?"

He pats the sides of my arms. "Now, that would be telling." He kisses my cheek, and I cringe just before he takes the seat opposite me.

"Please, gentlemen. Let us not stand on ceremony, shall we?"

Neil is the first one to reciprocate. "Never one to turn down a free meal. Especially not in the Temple."

After a few more moments, Luc reluctantly pulls out his chair. He sits right next to me, leg brushing mine. I sigh. Luc's just as stubborn and persistent as his brother. Does he know about Sky?

Comprised of every food group imaginable, the breakfast isn't complete without edible jewels or gold-carat leaves. Even the fruit has been cut and shaped into swan-like images while sugar Skeleton Flowers decorate other plates. Considering how many children go hungry every night, this meal should make my stomach want to drop, but it does just the opposite. Instead, the butterflies in my stomach have transformed into miniature dragons all roaring fire; they want to feast on my father's flesh.

Speak of the vampire himself, Force pours himself another glass of champagne from a second bottle crusted in diamonds and real pearls before opening the discussion. "Serenity, now you've shed your old face, I see your appetite is even more voracious than before."

"In more ways than one," I say, flashing a smile before sipping some water, preferring to remain sober.

"It seems both my children are similar." He sneers before leaning back to survey Neil and adding, "For quite different reasons, however."

I must look past Luc to see my half-brother on the other side with his cheeks stuffed full of doughnut—edible glitter and powdered sugar smeared on his lips. "What?" Shrugging, he says, "I'm just here for the food."

Rolling my eyes, I ignore him before helping myself to a clump of juicy grapes. I do my best to ignore Luc, who is far too close on my left side. When we both reach for the fruit bowl at the same time, his arm brushes mine. It doesn't feel like a shock. It feels like an annoyance. Some pest I must swipe at to claim my strawberries.

"I'd consider it a favor if you didn't inflict any personal harm on my guest, Serenity," Force addresses me, gesturing to my hand that's shoving Luc's out of the way.

I sit back, slouch, and cross my arms over my chest. "I'll try to keep that in mind." I pop a berry in my mouth.

"Hmm…" my father muses. "Some interesting developments must have taken place to breed this animosity. Such a shame. I was going to give him a fair chance."

Luc bristles beside me, and I snort. "Fair chance for what?"

"For your road to womanhood. Naturally."

I read right through the shimmery smile on his face. My father is serious. Unfortunately, he has reflexes like mine because he manages to catch the knife I've just thrown at his head. I follow up my action by pounding my fist on the table and rising.

"How. Dare. You?"

"What? It's not such an outlandish notion."

My father doesn't bat an eye. In fact, he enjoys the game even more by twisting the handle of the knife around and around with its point digging into the table.

"After all," Force points out, indicating Luc, "he did auction off the entire Aviary for your freedom. And from what my sources have unearthed, he also saved your life on multiple occasions.

Despite my obvious chagrin at losing, I respect Director Aldaine a great deal."

"Former director," I elucidate.

"Oh, once a director, always a director. Besides, I think he will come in quite handy for the plans I have in store for you, my little swan." He dabs at his mouth.

I glance over at Luc, but as per the norm, he's unreadable. Unlike my father who dons his emotions like a ring master. All pomp and circumstance.

"You see, I've hired Luc as my master artisan of the Penthouse as it were. Under my supervision, he will bring my vision for the Faces of the Temple to life!"

I step back too fast, knocking over my chair. It's been far too long since I growled, and the snarl works its way up my throat and vaults straight for Luc. Even after everything we've gone through, he still hasn't had enough. He still wants to imprison me in the lines and contours of his digital pages, dress me up and pretend I'm his little doll. He still refuses to let me go.

My nails ache to maul his skin like they once had. Leave permanent scars this time, but Neil stops me. My brother gets his arms around me and drags me away from the table, away from Luc.

"Can't you see this is what he wants?" Neil mutters in my ear, referring to our DNA's common heritage.

"Neil, if you—"

"Try to settle down and remember *exactly* what he said."

My brain skitters over my father's words just as my eyes settle on him. Judging by the bemused expression on his face, he's enjoying my little display. I reflect on his words, noting a change in one of them. The *Faces* of the Temple. Not just the Face.

I march around the table to confront my father. "Where is she?"

He swirls the liquid around in his glass. "Your mother or sister? It's so difficult to ascertain your thought processes."

"Then, I'll spell it out for you." I snatch up his glass, then chuck the champagne right into his face before leaning over and narrowing my eyes. "*Both*."

My father half-sighs, half-groans before sweeping a few droplets off his collar, though he ignores the champagne remnants rolling down his cheeks. Slowly, he scoots out of his chair.

He waves a hand to the two men. "Would you excuse us for a few moments, gentlemen? I wish to have a word alone with my daughter."

Neil is the one who reassures a hesitant Luc. "Come on, lover man. It's going to happen at some point. Better let them get it done and over with. Let 'em hash it out alone."

Luc's eyes don't stray from mine. He doesn't turn around once. Walks backward all the way to the door, nods to me, and closes it behind him. Sky would never leave. Not unless he was carried out.

My father sighs, his eyes zeroing in on me. Somehow, he's sucked out all the playfulness. He's left with a dark hysteria shimmering in those green orbs. What he does next is anything but slow. Before I can so much as blink, my father has pinned my arm behind my back and forced me against one of the glass windows.

"Look down, Serenity," he murmurs in my ear, voice bordering on seductive. "Long way to fall. I remind myself every time I wake up."

When I try to struggle, he just twists my arm farther, yanking a cry from my throat.

"Look," he commands, pressing my face harder into the glass. "You think I'm here to play games. Perhaps you are right. But a man with all this at his disposal never folds and always holds the right cards. And you—" He brushes the curls out of my face, then rubs his lips on my cheek to finish. "You are my royal flush. Whether you like it or not, you are my seed, my blood, my *essence*. You are the child I've waited seventeen years for. You will bring my Temple to its pinnacle. With you at my side, I will become the most infamous director of all time. I will obliterate the very founder. I know a queen when I see one, and I will do whatever it takes to help you become that queen."

He lets go of me so quickly I tumble to the floor. My arm still smarts from his assault, but he's not quite finished yet. No, Force squats beside me, wiping my hair to one side of my face so he may cup my chin and stare me down.

"I'm not looking for your love. I don't need it. But I am the head of the Syndicate, the director of the Temple, and your father first and foremost. You *will* respect me, daughter."

I jerk my chin away. "Respect for *what*? For every scar on my mother's back? For every night she spent screaming from her nightmares of this place? For you hunting us nonstop?"

Force curves one corner of his mouth. "Your mother has always been my Unicorn. Part of what completes me. We all have our roles in this world."

"What are you going to do?"

"You and your sister will be my Faces. You will be my dark and light. My night and day. My sun and moon. My life and death. My Yin and Yang."

My father takes me by the arm, then jerks me up. "You want to see her? Come on then, little Yang. Let us go meet your Yin."

Three

ReuNion

Bliss

$\mathcal{M}$Y MOTHER STILL DOESN'T TALK about my sister. At first, I believed it was out of grief. Or longing. But every time my father gives us the wee hours of the morning when I'm not tending to clients, her eyes come to life when I enter the Breakable Room. Like she's an ancient cathedral bell chiming for the first time. I've never encountered anything like it. It's why I want to run every time our eyes connect. She seems to understand too much. Not once has she tried anything more than cupping my cheek like she had that first day. She must know touch is my trigger. She's trying to nudge her love into me. Not force it.

I should tell her there's no use.

Numbness is better than love. Better than hope. It makes me strong enough for the Temple.

At times, I catch her body language mimicking mine. I can't deny our similarity. We are both quiet. Most of the time, we say nothing. She knows I'm giving simple companionship because it's all I can offer. Even to my mother. She accepts the emotional crumbs.

We sit with our backs against the glass, our legs curled into our chests, shoulders barely brushing, heads still on the wall behind us. Hands restless. Always anticipating the next client, my fingers aren't used to a lull. This place has worn her down. Like thin paper, she's folding in on herself again, remembering the creases and shape of what she used to be years ago.

"Do you want to ask me anything?"

It's the first question she's asked me. I didn't expect it to be a question that offers rather than seeks.

"Why did you leave me?"

There is no resentment in my voice. Resentment's chain is far too tiring to drag around for years. Loss is too heavy to cart on one's shoulders. I banished those emotions years ago, traded them in for my mountain of body parts instead. Now, I am simply *curious*.

"I had two choices. I could have you both in my life, but had to accept it would never be real. I would have needed to break Kerrick's heart. I couldn't play the Unicorn anymore. It would have destroyed me. And the girls I'd carried wouldn't truly be mine. Force would never have let me be a mother. Just a Unicorn on call every day…all day. So, I chose half a heart over no heart at all. And ever since, I've never stopped fighting to see you again."

She didn't need to add the last part. Nothing has come as a surprise. All words I'd suspected but I'd wanted to confirm regardless.

"Kerrick changed me. He made me stronger and weaker. I think that's what love means. Willing to be weak. You don't need to show it to the world—you just need to show weakness to one person."

She relates portions of her past but keeps them at a safe distance. They must be a special kind of private for her. Just like the mountain inside of me.

"I spent months resisting him. He showed me his weaknesses first. Sometimes, that's how it works. My moment didn't come until I was pregnant with you and your sister. Those were the only months your father left me alone for the most part. I couldn't keep anything down. And Kerrick was always there. Following me into the bathroom every time to hold my hair back. I didn't trust any man who touched me. I believed there was a hidden motive."

I nod in understanding. Even if it comes from good intentions, there is always an ulterior motive.

"Would you like to know the first moment I let him in?" my mother asks, turning her head toward mine.

I don't really want to, but I've swallowed enough in my time. Nothing much affects me anymore. I can take this just like I take everything.

"Would you believe I missed your father? He spent much of his time away on business during my pregnancy. His way of passing the time because he didn't want to jeopardize the twins. But he was my world. He was my purpose and my identity. I didn't know how to play a mother. It was never expected of me. Sickness didn't help either. I felt like it was my fault. That I must have committed some heinous crime to be feeling so miserable. Not performed the way he wanted. Then, I felt you kick."

My mother pauses, looks at her hands, and smiles. "It felt like some little war was going on inside me. It hurt. But it was the first time the pain made me feel *different*. Suddenly, this pain was from something amazing my body was creating. It made me feel empowered because I enjoyed the pain for myself instead of enjoying my pain for Force. It was the first time I recognized my body was capable of something other than being the Unicorn. Serafina came back to life. And I wanted someone to see *me*."

"Kerrick..." I say the name in no more than a whisper.

She nods. "I can't describe the expression on his face when I let him touch my belly. His eyes were gentle like silk roses. Nothing like your father's. During those days, I was just a vessel carting around his precious cargo. But not for Kerrick. To him, I was more like a beautiful puzzle box. Something he had to work long and hard to unravel because anything good in this world requires effort. To Kerrick, the treasure wasn't just the life inside me—it was my heart."

I can sense my mother's story is over. On some level, I want to feel happy for her, but I can't summon up that emotion. Especially not considering where she is now and what will eventually become of her. I can't imagine it was worth it. Staying behind would have been the safer option. In any case, I suppose it's good to have some insight into my mother's past. At least it puts a story to the photograph I've spent years looking at.

There's a small sense of anxiety she will try to apply her story to my own life. That she'll don a maternal hat and tell me there is hope for me—or someone out there who will love me—but she doesn't. Serafina lets the silence fill up the room. That is...good.

For some reason, my father doesn't cut our time off. So, my

mother and I linger in the empty room. Words slip out every now and then. Serafina seems to recognize that not even a herd of wild flying horses could drag a word out of me. I haven't had much use for talking over the years. My clients aren't too interested in my words. Only my body. Of course, I know all the right words necessary for any situation.

After another hour or two passes, my father finally opens the door. I almost sigh at the invasion of sound because the quiet is a welcome reprieve.

We both stand at the new presence.

A sigh catches in my throat as soon as he murmurs to someone behind him before urging the figure into the room, hand on the small of her back. Her movements are so flighty my eyes must race to catch up with her. I can almost imagine swan wings growing from her shoulders with the right shifting of light.

She stops short. Inertia should cause her to tumble forward, shouldn't it? Her eyes dash back and forth between us. They settle on me. Every feature is similar. Same eye shape, yet her expressions remind me of Father. She puts a bad taste in my mouth. There is no armor in her stance. She doesn't guard herself whatsoever. But I register something else—she may move like our father and have his eyes, but she does not stare at me the same way. No, her gaze is more like Serafina's, but unhindered and unbound. Like her emotions are bursting. Like she's ready to lunge for me and hug me hard.

And she does.

I don't hug her back. How could she expect me to? Her body may hold my identical DNA, but she is little more than a ghost to me.

Serenity is not my sister.

When she turns with no offense at my chilly indifference to embrace our mother, I note their bond. Rooted. Like invisible vines kissing one another. I become an infant again, fading into the background, too weak to breathe, needing a ventilator. Even if Serafina's always been an illusion, I've managed to clear the fog away. Now, it returns with abandon. It consumes me, creating a film over my eyes because I could never share what they have.

I never will.

Four

ReVenge SerVed CoLd

SERENITY

WANT TO YANK MY MOTHER out of this room. With each passing moment, it's becoming more cramped. Behind me, Neil enters alongside Luc, though I can't imagine what my father's motive is. It makes me even angrier since this moment should only belong to my family and no one else.

Family.

I contemplate that word when I peer at my sister, twisting my head from my mother's warm shoulder so I can see Bliss. She seems more like a mirage standing so still, but her hands never pause. Maybe that's the one bit of chaos she's taken from our father, but then I deny it because there's a rhythm to them. They are waiting. Waiting for what? Certainly not me. I confirm that when I step toward her, but she doesn't lift her head or so much as acknowledge my presence. Like I'm no more than a moth to her.

"Serenity." My mother draws my attention back to her.

I shake my head, staring at my mother. Does she know I'm checking her for bruises? Whether she does or not, she doesn't hide from me. It's a new dynamic because she spent all my life hiding everything from me, protecting me. Maybe she understands parents shouldn't always try to protect their children from the truth.

Content when I find no bruises or marks on her, I turn around and march right to Force, but I jerk a finger to Luc and Neil.

"What are *they* doing here? I want to see my father now. My *real* father!"

My father brings a fist to his chin, musing aloud, "They are

19

here for a purpose, but I am curious what power you think you have to give orders? Especially here?"

I do a double-take before glancing around.

"Don't you know where you are, Serenity?"

When I don't respond, my father extends a hand to Bliss. A shock-wave stuns the butterflies in my stomach when she accepts. Revulsion sours the wave even more when he slides a hand around her waist and then motions to our environs.

"Perhaps you'd like to enlighten her, Mara."

Why does he call her Mara? There's a history here I don't know. I'm already getting a sense the past seventeen years are about to be packed into the next few days I will share with Bliss. Except my mother and I have always shared a bond. Bliss and I share nothing but our DNA. Will that be enough?

"This is the Breakable Room."

Bliss's voice is mysterious. Like some window covered in a thousand layers of winter frost. How could I ever hope to reach her?

"It is the oldest room in the Penthouse, and it was the original client room. The Temple's founding father found inspiration here, and the urban legend is the original Glass District owner coined the term 'Breakables' in this room because everyone inside it always breaks."

"Very good, Mara."

"We get it, Daddy-O," Neil huffs while crossing his arms over his chest. "This is the place you'd always bring Serafina to have 'your way' with her. Get to the point."

Force chortles just a little, eyeing the young man standing in the entryway beside a grim Luc. "Bluntly put, son. And despite how much I'm enjoying this buildup, I believe you are right for once in your pathetic existence. It is time to get to the point."

My father mentally activates the technology inside his brain that connects him to the Temple network. After, he states, "Send him in."

Less than a minute later, the Breakable door opens. One more familiar face emerges. Even though I'm closer, my mother reaches him before me. I find myself stopping short of them so my parents may reunite first. Kerrick's hands aren't even bound. Instead, they roam my mother's face, touch her skin, and rub away the tears on her cheeks. Finally, they cup her face as he leans in to kiss her. I notice my 'father's' expression. I expect him to cringe, to wrinkle his nose, or to roll his eyes, but he does none of this. He simply stands with hands casually folded behind his back as he studies the three of us once I join my parents.

Kerrick's arms are long enough to hold us both. This is what matters. We are so close I can feel their heartbeats pumping against my chest. I breathe in the scent of my *real* father. Nothing has changed. No bruises defile his skin. His strong arms are just as composed as ever. They hold more of my mother than me, which is just the way it should be. I'm not jealous. Right now, I'm standing beneath the one glowing lantern on a dark night. This is our bit of home in the glassy Temple.

Our circle would be more complete with Sky, but it's not broken without him. He's just another curve that sits on top, just lingering on the edge.

Kerrick is the first one to break the silence. Part of me wants to interrupt him, delay whatever Force has planned, but this should be my real father's moment. He's spent years cleaning up after Force. It's now time for him to confront the vampire who took so much of his wife's life from her.

"You always have an agenda," Kerrick growls, stepping forward with fist braced.

They are equally matched. Kerrick has always been tall, but he and Force are the same height. Kerrick's body is still muscle-packed. Not as much as it was while I was growing up, but he's always tended to his muscles over the years. It wouldn't take much for him to bring my biological, silver-spoon father down *physically*. But mentally, Force is ready with cards he is dying to play. There's anticipation in his uninhibited stride. His body swings back and forth as he approaches Kerrick, sizing him up. More than anything, I want to step forward to confront him, but I've already done my part. This is Kerrick's moment. I'm not about to ruin it.

"I don't care what it is," Kerrick spits the words. "You will not hurt my family ever again."

My father's laugh is expected. It bobs, skips, and bounces, ricocheting off the walls around us as he begins to circle Kerrick.

"Right you are, Kerrick. I never will hurt your family because they are not *your* family. They never were. And they never will be."

My father rounds Kerrick's side. That's when I catch the glint of the object. Kerrick is too late in turning around. I'm too late in lunging. In this moment, he is Force incarnate. He is not the director of the Temple. When he grabs my father by the hair, yanking his head back so he may slash one thin line with the knife, so he may paint blood across Kerrick's throat, Force is the head of the Syndicate.

"*No!*"

My scream should shatter the earth. It should burst all the glass walls so I can get my hands around one chunk. I've never been fast enough. Blood licks up what's left of my real father's life threads, snapping them one by one as it spills all over the glass floor. He was the calm in our vortex. Our balance. Our compass. Our touchstone. We can't touch Kerrick anymore.

Even without a glass chunk, I lunge for my father. Luc is closing in on my heels, but Force is more than ready. He doesn't even let my mother reach her husband's side. He doesn't let her tears mingle with his blood before seizing her by the waist and dragging her against his chest. He coils one hand—the one holding the knife—around her throat. Smearing Kerrick's blood against her skin, he kisses her jaw directly beneath her ear, cooing words I cannot hear just before wagging one finger at Luc and me.

"Ah, ah, ah," he warns us before we can take a step forward. "Trust me, Serenity. I am more than certain you could kill me in this moment. I recognize it. It's what I've waited all these years to witness. But what you and Director Aldaine must understand is an old proverb—*when you go out for revenge, you must dig two graves.* In this case, the second grave would be your mother's."

Through gritted teeth, I say, "What are you talking about?"

"Sweet Serafina," my father murmurs, rubbing his mouth against the side of her head. She shivers against him. "You never disappoint. You should have learned years ago you can never run from me. I will always find you. Our hearts have always beat as *one.* This time, it has more meaning."

He directs his attention back to us. "I've equipped your mother with the same type of technology Jade used in the Garden.

Except I took it to a much grander level. Serafina's heart is directly connected with mine. Our heartbeats are more synchronized than ever. Mine beats. Hers beats. Mine flatlines. Hers flatlines."

Releasing my mother, he chucks her to the floor. He wipes the knife blade on his own clothes before approaching me. All I can see is my mother and the way her fingers curl around Kerrick's lifeless head, careless of his blood staining the ends of her dress.

I want to bite my father's hand when it cups my shoulder, but I whip around.

"You wanted a reunion, Serenity. How does it sit with you?" he asks, smile toying with me.

"Someday, somehow, I will kill you." I don't threaten. It's a promise. "Nothing on earth could ever keep me from killing you."

Force leans in to whisper in my ear. "If you do, I'll be sure to wait for you and we can stroll down to hell together."

Five

OuR FaCes

BLISS

I DON'T KNOW WHAT TO SAY or do. It isn't the first time I've seen my father kill. It isn't the first time I've smelled blood. But it is the first time my stomach has lurched. Not from the sight of the blade. Not from Serenity's hair-raising scream. Not from the life seeping out of Kerrick's eyes. The lurching comes when I see my mother shrink into herself. I can see the effort in her eyes, the way she's fighting so hard not to cry. Like she wants to catch all the tears that escape and send them back. Or how she forces herself to stare at the crumpled body of her husband, pretending he's just a ghost. Nothing works. Everything is too sudden for her. She hasn't had enough time to build up her armor again. In some ways, she lost most of it thanks to the lifeless man on the floor.

And the man gripping her now has ripped her heart right open. She's bleeding. My father is an expert in making people bleed. Both inside and out.

He chose this room. Planned for the witnesses. Not only due to his desire for an audience but to usurp his dominance. This is his Temple after all. Slitting Kerrick's throat in front of Serafina's daughters is the gateway, the doorway for my mother to become the Unicorn once again. We cannot escape our pasts. Our ghosts never leave us. Even when we try to deny their existence, we keep them closer than anyone else. They are part of us.

I understand the two men here are for Serenity's sake. Neil doesn't move, but he does drag a hand through his hair. A help-

24

less hand. A son who outgrew trying to please his father long ago. Instead, he put as much distance as he could between him and the Temple. Except I know Neil brought the Temple with him to each international modeling shoot, every lingerie-stuffed boudoir, every paradisiacal body-painted beach.

When the other man advances to join Serenity, I pause to study him. Curious at his closeness to her, I tilt my head to the side, more interested in him than my father's words because they are always the same. The man standing next to Serenity now is no lover, no client. I recognize him. The Aviary director. Like my father, he reeks of power, but he wears it in a subtler way. In some ways, he reminds me of Neil, though I can't imagine why. Something in the curves of each hand, but his eyes are a fierce contradiction. With just one glance, I can tell he has killed before. Unlike Serenity's, his eyes are not senseless wrath. They are etched in purpose. He knows just how to sink his brows low and tighten the muscled seams into more than a threat—a threatening promise.

I remember her final Swan dive. His proximity to Serenity is more than understandable now. Rumors have escalated throughout the Boroughs ever since the auction. Serenity and Luc have become the modern-day Romeo and Juliet, a veritable pair of star-crossed lovers, though they seem more storm-tossed to me.

Only when my father touches Serenity do I pause from my study of Director Aldaine. I can't hear what my father tells her. All I see is her reaction. Her fighter instinct is so potent and so childish—the innocent, golden child he's always wanted. The radiant sun to my bitter moon.

"Mara, would you please escort your sister to her room?"

Stoic as ever, I step toward a shell-shocked Serenity, but she throws her body back from Force and refuses, "I won't leave her!"

"Yes, you will." Force doesn't allow any argument. "Whether you want to or not, you will. I'm giving your mother a little time alone to grieve. We have unfinished business, you see."

She gnashes her teeth and raises her hand, but he only chuckles and reminds her of the connected heart device.

"I can certainly have you dragged out," he offers. "We can do this the easy way or the hard way."

Serenity doesn't bat an eye when she blows a curl out of her face, narrows her eyes, and utters, "I *never* do things the easy way."

"And I love you all the more for it, my beautiful daughter."

He sends for two guards, who arrive and lock their hands around her arms.

"No marks," my father reminds them.

I truly don't understand her logic or her mindset. Why this pointless exhibit? He always gets his way. I sway past Luc, whose eyes pause from Serenity for just one moment to look upon me. No amount of curiosity, nor judgment. Our gazes don't linger on one another's, but somehow, I still sense his eyes on me when I turn my back to follow the guards pulling along a thrashing Serenity.

"Never a dull moment, eh, sissies?" Neil remarks on our way out the door.

"Shut up!" Serenity kicks one leg up, aiming for his groin.

He curses when it connects, doubling over just a little.

I pat him on his shoulder. "Never a dull moment indeed."

Six

FaCes of the TemPle

SERENITY

"WHY DID YOU DO THAT?" It's the first question out of my sister's mouth when we arrive in my bedroom. Rather, when I was forced.

I'm confused. "Do what?"

"Why did you bother with the guards? It was going to happen either way. Just like he said. It didn't matter."

"It wasn't for him. It was for me. It mattered to me," I defend myself before slumping onto the bed, wanting Sky's warmth more than ever. The weather inside me has changed. Frost cakes my butterflies' heads. As everything starts to sink in, I imagine there will be snow and then ice.

Bliss doesn't respond. All she does is stand there in the center of the room without saying anything, hands all fidgety. Just like my mother. A million different secrets must breed inside Bliss, too. Growing up, there were times I could steal glimpses of my mother's, but I doubt that will happen with Bliss. Nor do I think she will be obliging to share.

"Why does he call you Mara?" It seems like a simple question, a fair one.

"Because he made a mistake. I was never meant to be Bliss. He confused me with someone else."

With me.

"Why doesn't he just change it?"

"My legal name is Bliss. He kept it as a reminder so he would never stop searching for what he sought most—his ultimate hap-

27

piness."

Her words are pointed facts. Nothing more. That is the way she sounds. The way she looks—ghostly like my mother. Not all there. I wonder if her mind is caught somewhere in limbo, halfway between fantasy and reality so she doesn't really have to deal with either. Far too extreme for that, I've managed to bring my fantasy world with me into reality. My lightning diffuses fantasy when necessary—like when I interact with my father. I don't dissociate; I daydream. For the first time, I consider how daydreaming could be a form of dissociation.

Bliss says nothing else, just nods at me before turning to make her way back to the staircase.

"Will you return?" I ask just before she leaves. I don't delay her too much. I need Sky.

"If you wish, we could certainly have a meal together sometime. I suppose it's best since we'll be working alongside each other soon."

I straighten. "What do you mean?"

She purses her lips as if she's weighing how much to tell me. "Perhaps he hasn't had time to give you more information. Tonight, I wager. I shouldn't say anything."

"You don't have to do everything he tells you to." *You don't have to do anything*, I want to tell her.

"I am not you, Serenity."

Just as Bliss starts to descend the staircase, I hear other footsteps overlap hers. It's followed by a low murmur of 'good girl' about halfway down.

"I thought you weren't coming back until dinner." I sneer upon my father's approach.

"I enjoy playing the unpredictable. Besides, I have a few minutes before I meet with some business clients. I decided it would be a good opportunity to tell you a few things."

He has no respect for personal privacy or space. My skin turns into one giant ice block when he sits on the bed next to me, then places his hand on my knee. My automatic reaction is to shrink away.

"It had to happen this way. Surely you recognize that. He could never exist because blood is everything. Family is everything.

28

And he was merely an undocumented trespasser. There was no other fate for him but death."

Is Sky listening right now? If he is, I can't have him try to attack. Not with knowing what will happen to my mother.

"And you made sure I couldn't secure your death in the process," I launch the words right at him.

"I am an incredibly good predictor of such situations. I allow no room for error. Having linked your mother's heart with mine offers me reassurance. And time."

"Time for what?"

"For me to train you."

I back away from him even more until my spine is flat against the bed frame. "What makes you think I will listen to you? What makes you think I will do anything for you?"

"Hmm…" Force smirks as if contemplating some prior plan he's about to unearth. "You think I have no more tricks up my sleeve?" He clicks his tongue. "You should know I can squeeze blood from steel if I wish. And judging from your performance in the Aviary, I trust my offer will be accepted."

"What offer?"

"I will give you my word and follow through with the action of not taking your mother to my bed if you agree to my conditions. You will let me show you my world and train you to become one of my Faces of the Temple."

I hug my knees to my chest, wanting more information. "What are the Faces of the Temple? I've only heard urban myths, but it's never been done before."

"Unlike other Museums that cater to a certain theme, The Temple is not limited. It was the first Museum, and it holds the rights for any theme. Every single girl in this Temple is placed on a certain level. Very few ever move up. Your mother was one of those blessed few. Tomorrow, I will introduce you to my empire and all we display here."

"Get to the point."

"Unlike all other girls here, Serenity, you and Mara are gifted with an extraordinary talent—and an extraordinary passion."

He segregates the terms so I know good and well the latter belongs to me.

"Mara has spent much of her life honing her talents. Here, you will hone your passion into whatever guise I choose. You will perform on any and every level of the Temple. And I will ensure your displays are as public as I can make them."

"That's why you hired Luc."

"I appreciate his vision and his taste. I look forward to seeing what other wonders he will produce in you."

"And what about Mara?"

"All these years, Mara has performed in private for certain clients. I have been waiting a long time to unveil both of you. However, you will perform separately. Only the cost of an interaction will see you both together."

"Interaction?" I immediately stiffen at the word. Performances are one thing. But if he thinks I'm going to interact, I'll bite his finger off right now. I might not be able to kill him, but all my butterflies' wings are vibrating at the thought of the pain I could inflict on him.

"Mara functions on a level of interaction skill far higher than yours. That is why I will keep your dual interactions simple. It will still function as a display but more of an up close and personal one." My father leans over and touches my cheek. "My Yin and Yang interaction."

"Why the Yin and Yang?"

"My life has been off-balance for too long." He lifts his chin, but his gaze wanders. "From an early age, I sought out happiness at every turn. I was denied nothing. The world was my oyster."

He taps a finger to my nose. "But as I grew older, I gave up childhood lust pursuits and spent years trying to achieve the ultimate control. It's why I became this powerful and profitable. But happiness was still out of my reach. Control still hung on the point of a knife. My only sense of relief came in the moments shared with your mother."

"Don't you dare talk about my mother, you sick scumbag. You could never deserve her even if you crawled all the way from hell to heaven."

"Exactly, Serenity." He grins before capturing a few of my curls, then rubbing them between his fingers. "She was my opposite in every way. My balance. A sense of order in all the chaos that is the

EMILY SHORE

Temple's world. Serafina is the closest I've ever come to euphoria."

He pauses, lets out a sigh. "But I've always been aware of my mortality. Nothing lasts forever…except one thing. And that is legacy. Everything I've experienced, everything I've learned over the years, everything I've worked so hard to amass—it would be pointless without the opportunity to pass it on to someone. That someone would have to be incredibly special." His eyes target mine. "That someone couldn't merely be trained. That someone would have to be born. Like me, that someone would have to possess that thirst from birth, that drive, and that fire."

"It's not fire. It's *lightning*," I correct him, at once wishing I could grab the words and shove them back inside my throat. They should be mine.

My father raises his brows, clearly pleased by my retort. "Lightning," he repeats. "So fitting for the two of us. But I have yet to hear your answer."

Closing my eyes, I inhale deeply and then blow out through my nostrils. "If you keep my word and leave my mother alone, I'll let you train me as much as you want to."

After enduring Jade in the Garden, I feel better equipped to handle whatever my father will bring to the table.

"I'll be your Face of the Temple. I'll perform however you want me to," I go on but raise a hand before he can express his approval. "But I won't agree to your *interaction*, no matter it is. My body belongs to me. I'll be damned if anyone else but the one I choose gets close to it."

"Ahh yes, another prospect we must sort out. Understand, Serenity, the olive branch I am extending to you. Mara had no such fortune favored on her. But you are different." He tucks my hair behind my ear even as I flinch. "Rest assured, I will bring scores of suitors to the table, but ultimately, I will let the final choice remain in your hands. You may choose one or you may choose multiple. You may keep one or you may keep more. Whatever you decide will be in your power."

All my butterflies are stuck in the thick bile in my stomach. Somehow, I manage to keep it there so it doesn't rise to the surface. As much of a relief it is, the whole idea of it is unfair and ridiculous because it should be every girl's choice. It should be Bliss's

31

choice, too.

"You're wasting your time."

"We will see. For now, I accept your terms. I will not bed your mother, and short of my interaction assignment, you will complete your duties as the Face of the Temple."

"For now?" I look up as he rises, hanging on his two previous words.

"Come now, daughter." He grins, the devil dancing in the seams of his supple mouth. "You don't think I'll give up that easily, do you? After all this time, I'm not about to let my vision slip from my fingers. You've agreed to only part of it. But my Yin and Yang will be fulfilled one way or another."

I hiss, "Not without my say so."

"Then, I suppose I will have to change your mind." Placing one hand on the bed frame above my head, he leans over to assure me, "I am very good at that, you know."

My father turns to leave.

"You know I hate you, don't you?" I say just after he's reached the staircase.

"Yes." He turns just his head. "Fascinating how closely the lines of love and hate touch one another. I doubt there will ever be a middle ground between us such as Mara and I share. And that suits me perfectly.

"The rest of the day is yours to do with as you wish," he instructs while rounding the glass staircase down to the first level. "You may go anywhere in the Penthouse you desire, except for the Breakable Room, of course. I'll return for dinner. Enjoy your day, Serenity."

AS SOON AS MY FATHER is gone, I race for the vent, but Sky has opened it already and drops into my room. Before he even rises from his instinctive crouch, I throw my arms around him. Instead of raising me up, Sky sinks low with me, welcoming how my body curls into his. He lets me contort into a petite little ball that shakes and sobs and whimpers into his chest until he smells less like Sky and more like my salty tears. In and out of seconds and minutes, he never speaks. Just a fortress of muscles that shields me from anything that might interfere with my grief over the father I've lost. That *we've* lost. Kerrick was the counselor. Sky is the protector. This is what he does best.

I pick through the memories of my *real* father as if they are different magical objects stored in jars. A laser bullet for the times Kerrick took me to the VirtuRoom in one of the hotels we visited. Laser tag on steroids with volumetric targets that would interact with one another. I lost to Kerrick every time. Sky was always better than me, but time with my father was what mattered most.

Sky lets me break the silence first. I do with my cheek still tucked into his chest. "It happened so quickly. Right there in front of all of us. He cut his throat like it was nothing."

That's when I feel a rocking sensation beneath me. A trembling. I tilt my head up to see Sky's head bowed, waves trampling his brow as a soundless tear drops down his cheek. For years, Sky and Kerrick had a deep relationship. A bond I could never understand but one that united them and caused them to spend hours every day training. My real father equipped Sky with what he needed to keep me safe in his absence. Their shared responsibility. Kerrick taught Sky what it is to be a man and to respect a girl. Even if she happens to be a major pain in his ass at times.

I lean up to kiss the tear that's made its way to his jaw, but Sky brings his mouth down on mine instead. Closing my eyes, I let his hand wind around my neck, preventing me from any sort of escape even though I wouldn't consider it. We swap our grief back and forth. We taste each other's loss, trading heartache. When Sky deepens, hardens the kiss, I reciprocate and grip his collar, understanding how we're sampling just the edge of our shared wrath. He gives me thunder; I give him lightning. Neither wants to pull away. So, we do it slowly. A brush of his mouth on my chin, my nose nuzzling his cheekbone, his forehead brushing mine, my mouth landing on his neck. At last, we're ready to put a small gap between us. Too much for Sky, who covers the sides of my face with his hands. Too much for me, so I plant my fingers on his bare collarbone.

"I should have known you'd found a way inside."

The new voice shatters our moment like a dropped snow globe. Sky shoots up, flexing his muscles before marching straight over to Luc and driving him far up against the wall with one hand secured around his throat.

"How dare you? How dare you push your way back into her life again? What do you think you're going to accomplish?"

That's when I remember my father's words about hiring Luc.

Luc doesn't get a chance to answer because I yank Sky's hair. Hard enough for him to break his hold. I'm not about to defend Luc. I'm about to defend myself.

Putting myself between them, I raise a finger to Sky. "You know better than that! You heard everything. He wasn't even there when I agreed to my father's terms. You don't have a right to argue that."

"The hell I don't!" Sky looks down on me, casting his shadow over my face.

"Not with *my* mother's life in the balance," I add, which twists Sky's tongue into silence.

He grunts once, paces the floor, eyes darting to Luc and then back to me. "Why him?" He jerks a finger to his brother.

I roll my eyes. "Because I'd trust someone else my father would hire so much more? At least I know what to expect with him."

"Which is never knowing what to expect," Sky huffs.

I suppose I can't argue on that one.

"I came to offer you something else," Luc states as he comes away from the wall. "That is… if you two are finished talking about me while I'm still in the room."

Sighing, I open my hand. "Offer me what?"

"Access to my final draft before the process begins."

"I don't want it."

"Serenity—"

"Shut up, Sky," I snap, then refuse again. "I don't want it. The dynamic worked last time. We all know how well I performed in the Aviary. And the Garden. Only one thing has changed—I have to be even better."

Luc's brows sink but in confusion. "Why?"

Sky rolls his eyes. "Figure it out, brother."

For one second, Luc deadpans. Realization strikes, and Sky elbows me with a grin when Luc concludes, "You're planning on

34

escaping."

"Nothing gets by you, does it?" Sky says.

"I'll let him do the planning while I keep Force's eyes on me." I jerk my head toward Sky.

"And what about your mother? If the technology implant is what I suspect, then it has a surface-area limitation. One step outside Temple property—"

"Such a defeatist attitude," Sky interrupts. "Ever heard the old expression 'where there's a will, there's a way?'"

"There will only be a *way* if you two idiots can manage to work together," I don't neglect to add while huffing.

"And what about Bliss?" Luc asks. "She seems very content with her Temple life."

Yes, the one flaw with the plan. I won't leave without my sister, but I can't deny the truth of Luc's words. My father poisoned her from her first day here. Part of me fears I'll have to bleed the poison out of her very, very slowly.

Luc doesn't wait for an answer. "Your father has already given me instructions for tomorrow."

"So soon?" I purse my lips.

"He wishes to resurrect the Swan for your first public exhibit as one of the Temple Faces. It will be water-themed."

"What about Bliss?"

"She is Yin. The dark one. Her performances are not for the public. Only your interactions together will be public."

I shake my head. "I told him I wouldn't do any interactions."

"Force already set me to work preparing the interaction display. He is confident he will convince you before your performance tomorrow. Apparently, Neil has a bet going."

"Who's he betting on?" I ask above Sky's groan.

"You."

"Good. He'll win then."

Seven

Scars

Bliss

I BELIEVE IT'S HIS INTENTION TO leave her with the corpse for the rest of the day.

He's forbidden Serenity from entering the room again but not me.

I suppose I shouldn't have expected to find her in a different position. It's ironic, really. Seeing her on the floor with his blood staining parts of her dress, her thin form tucked into itself, but her eyes spread wider than Temple doors. I know she must have kept her dead husband's soul close to her heart. She's not empty without him. She's just less grounded.

I recognize the loss in her eyes. I've felt that same loss. In her case, she lost someone. In mine, I lost pieces of someone. And she can never return. Thousands of men trampling over one another replaced those pieces. No choice but to keep them with me—ghosts on my skin. To survive, I've simply made a mountain of them.

As I get closer, I consider how much younger she appears right now. Thanks to my father, I know Serafina was only fifteen when she bore her twins. I've done the math. In this moment, she is the child, and I am the mother. She is the novice, and I am the teacher.

I lower to the floor next to her, careful not to pick up any traces of blood.

She's coiled her hand up to her back just beyond her shoulder, pressing her fingers into the skin there. Conscious of her motivation but unsure of what to say, I remain where I am and wait on whether she decides to share.

After some time, she says, "He was the only other man to see my scars. But where Force created them, Kerrick was the one who made me see how they were *beautiful*. Meaningful."

I have no words for that. Mine have never been beautiful. They are all the same. Despite having so much of Serafina in me, it never helped Father to create new scars on me. Other men have admired his handiwork. They find their own creative, boundless ways to hurt my body even if Force allows none to hold a whip but himself. Part of me wonders if that will change. If he will teach Serenity.

I don't have time to ponder because the door to the Breakable Room opens.

Eight

DesSert BeFore DinNer

SERENITY

"I LOVE DESSERT BEFORE DINNER. ARE you the same?" my father calls to me from the lower level.

Sky is back in the rafters. Luc left in short order after our discussion earlier so he could formulate his artistry, his 'vision'. Spending most of the day with Sky was a sort of healing for us. Except healing takes longer than a day.

I slip my hand across the staircase railing as I respond, "I'm my father's daughter, aren't I?"

"Excellent!" He extends a hand to me once I've descended. "And I'm so happy to see you've dressed for the occasion."

Our banter drips with sarcasm. This will be a simple dynamic for me to slip into. I will play the role more effectively than with Luc because I know what to expect from Force. Where Luc always savored the moments where he saw the real Serenity, my father enjoys my performances. Dressing in the fine gown that looks more like silver filigree all along my curves is my way of playing along, all of which he recognizes, which thrills him.

"Hmm…" Force captures my chin, moving my head from side to side. "No makeup? You wound me."

"My face is enough on its own."

He secures my arm into his, linking them as he escorts me out of my bedroom. "But keeping up pretenses is so much more entertaining, I believe. Oh well, I suppose it will keep me in suspense until I witness your interaction. I do hope you will soon take advantage of all your room's amenities. I spared no expense."

He leans in to murmur, "N.A.I.L.S is such an incredible machine, and I ordered the latest version just for you."

I think of the body applicator. The thought of using it shouldn't feel so intimidating.

"And you'll discover your bed is equipped with a little something special." Force deepens his voice as he pats my hand. "No doubt you noticed the sprite light canopy. Sometimes, you should tap into the Pleasure Program—clever little name…" my father boasts as he leads me to the door, so I guess we will not be having dinner in my bedroom. "Let's just say I thought it would be a spectacular way to spoil my long-lost princess."

I'm not sure I even want to know.

After a few more minutes of suspenseful silence involving an elevator descent and a walk down a long and familiar hallway, we arrive at our destination—the frosted glass door.

"What's this?" I ask.

"Oh, dessert will be served in the Breakable Room tonight."

My father turns the knob, then ushers me inside.

This time, I'm surprised to see Bliss sitting on the floor beside my mother just inches from Kerrick's dead body. The sight of his corpse sends pure lightning up my spine, and I hug my arms before approaching my mother.

I don't get a chance to take more than a couple of steps when my father grips me by the arm, preventing me from going farther. Then, he raises a hand, signaling for Bliss to come.

"What is going on?" I screw my brows lower as she reaches my side.

"I promised you, Serenity," he says. "I am a man of my word. Mara, be a good girl and hold your sister still for me."

Bliss quickly follows his orders. Force wastes no time in withdrawing an object from his dinner jacket—a black leather whip. He glances at me to note my shocked eyes, grins, then steps toward my mother.

"Liar!" I thrust my whole body toward him, but it barely moves an inch.

Bliss is stronger than me? How can she be stronger?

"You liar," I scream. "Get away from her! You said you'd leave her alone."

My mother doesn't even move. Her eyes don't register surprise. It's as if she expected this.

He lifts an index finger. "I said nothing of the sort. I merely said I would not take her to my bed, and I will abide by those terms. And I did leave her alone for much of the day. Perhaps in the future, you should be clearer in regard to your specifications."

"Bastard!"

I try to escape again, but Bliss keeps her arms cemented around me in just the precise way. No matter how much I kick and buck against her, she remains resolute. Why? How can she stand there and watch this? That is *our* mother he's approaching. That is *our* mother he's raising the whip to. That is *our* mother who is not going to fight back.

"Mom." My voice breaks as I plead with her. "Please, you can—"

Force interrupts with a snigger. "Oh no, she can't, Serenity. Isn't that right, Serafina?" Bending, he drags one finger across her cheek. She shivers. "It's time to remind you of who you are. Time for you to become the Unicorn again."

"I'll be whatever you want, Force," she murmurs.

So much for knowing what to expect from Force. And my mother.

He raises the whip.

"Stop," I cry.

"Please, Serenity." He pauses to regard me, gesturing to Serafina. "You are interfering with my dessert."

"I'm going to do so much more than that. I'm going to spoil your appetite!" I wrestle against my sister when he twirls the whip.

He orders my sister again. "Hold her still."

Her grip on me wavers for one moment. It's the first time I've seen the ice in her eyes crack. A hairline fissure. The recognition—the *emotion*—there is plain as day. I seize hold of the moment, jerk out of her arms, and fling myself at my father, grabbing hold of the whip. When his hand retains its claim and our bodies fall into a tug of war, I raise my head to see my father smiling. Grinning from ear to ear.

"All you have to do is agree to my terms," he reminds me, giving the leather a sharp tug.

I yank back. "No!"

"Wait."

The voice startles us both because it comes from behind us. Not in front of us. It's so small. Just like our mother's. She steps forward, hands folded calmly in front of her.

"Father, will you hear another option that will satisfy everyone?"

I notice movement out of the corner of my eye. It's the first time Mom has moved. Does she know what Bliss is going to ask?

"Color me intrigued," our father muses. "Please, Mara, endow on us your superior alternative."

"Change the terms to give Serenity and me a dual interaction, but one where she is not touched. It will suit the roles of Yin and Yang because men always desire more what they cannot touch. It will encourage appetites. Will that settle you some?"

"Some," he agrees. "But my appetite remains unquenched."

He stares at our mother once more with a feral glint in his eye. I give the whip one more tug, and it comes free. I clutch it to my chest, denying him the sick pleasure he seeks.

"That is why I will play the Unicorn," my sister offers.

"*No*," Mum immediately cries in a hoarse voice as she tries to stand. Is that why she wasn't going to fight? Because she didn't want him to…

Force ignores her while considering Bliss's proposal. "It is an intriguing notion." He begins to pace.

"Force, no!"

She rushes toward him, and I want to hold her back. She can't do anything against him. His dominance. His control. Her sacrificial pleas are just giving him more reason to deny her because she's showing him another weakness. Another way of bleeding her by attacking the one thing she has left—her own daughters.

Force taps his mouth, playful smile curling the corners as he appraises Bliss. "I believe we shall up the ante, so to speak. While it would be a thrill to determine if I could achieve the same power I had with your mother with you, I know it would be a guarantee if I delegated that to Serenity."

My mother marches toward Force, but her eyes are pleading. "No," she croaks.

"I know you've handled the whip before, Serenity." My father ignores her, closing the distance between us. "Jade didn't have to tell me anything. I can tell by the way you grip it."

I brandish it. "I'd rather use it on you!"

Wagging a finger, he clicks his teeth. "Time to choose, my beloved girl. Your mother or your sister. If you agree to Mara's proposition, no man will touch you in an interaction. And I will sweeten the deal. Not only will I not bed Serafina nor turn her into my Unicorn, but I will also agree not to seduce her, manipulate her, or even speak to her unless she speaks to me first. Handing down my legacy to you is more of a thrill than I can imagine."

He pauses as I weigh the options back and forth. I glance at my mother, but she violently shakes her head. But I stare at both her and my sister. This is ridiculous. How can I choose? If I could take the whip instead I would, but swallowing an ocean would be easier.

What Bliss's motive is in all this, I can't fathom. All I know is that glimmer of emotion she showed. Some relationship between them must have developed in the weeks Force has kept my mother here. All I need is one look at Bliss to know she can take this. More capable than me.

It's obvious Mother doesn't want this. No real parent would. She'd rather take the whip. By nature, it's the parent who sacrifices for their children, who bears pain for them. Not the other way around. But my mother spent her entire life sacrificing for me, doing whatever it took to protect me—even from herself. She spent her entire life running from a man whose ghost followed her, hunted her like she was some stag. She spent her entire life searching for Bliss. And now, Kerrick's gone.

She's not strong enough to become the Unicorn again.

Am I strong enough? The lightning monster deep inside me rears its head, eager, snapping at my quickening butterflies. If I do this, I run the risk of sucking my father's poison. But I have faith it won't overcome me. Just as I have faith in Sky. Just as he has faith in me. It's time I prove to my mother she can, too. I will get us all out of here before I turn into the monster my father is.

By the way Force reacts, my silent nod could have been the hallelujah chorus.

Nine

Old PatTerns NeW InteRactIon

SERENITY

SHOULDN'T BE SURPRISED LUC OUTDID himself again.

Despite having an automatic-body applicator, my father prefers preparers to see to my exhibit. N.A.I.L.S is for daily life.

My preparer sets to work on painting my body after she's finished molding the gown onto my skin. She is a silly young woman. Only a few years older than me. To her, this is a career and nothing more. Belinda doesn't savor the art; she hurries through it. The only reason my father selected her is due to her lightning-fast hands that can fulfill quotas. Quantity and quality are both important to the Temple when it comes to the higher levels, though Belinda operates on all. Her equally fast tongue prattles on, complaining she has dozens more girls to design tonight—something about how she's more of a hot commodity than the ones she paints.

Never once does she appraise me like I am a canvas.

As usual, the gown preparation takes place behind a dressing screen before Belinda places me before a three-way mirrored vanity.

I adopt a serene expression as she rolls her eyes and mutters, "Workhorse. That's what I am. Nothing better to do than make you pretties up all day. If they make me keep this up, I won't have hands anymore!"

After she does my eye makeup, she applies a shimmery white glitter that encompasses my brow's surrounding area and sweeps down to my cheekbone. Her next act is to attach tiny feather wisps to the outer curves of my lashes. They curl upward, teasing the air above my brow when I open my eyes. She applies a temporary tattoo of a tiny swan on each side of my face just on the corner of the eye, mimicking a tear. I'm almost dumbfounded when the swans begin to move, lightly fluttering their wings. A digital temporary tattoo shouldn't be too much of a surprise.

The gown itself is comprised of feathers. My father has ordained elements of both the Swan and Skeleton Flower into this costume, and Luc's precise vision comes to life in hundreds of swan feathers interlaid over one another. Sealed tight across my lethal curves.

Revealing more expertise, Belinda adds tiny swan-like symbols to my center midriff since the feathers have parted ways at the base of my throat, plunging in a deep vee all the way down to my navel, leaving the inner curves of my cleavage exposed. The open panel effect is too much skin for my taste, but thanks to the Swan and the Skeleton Flower, I find myself accepting it. Feathers coat the sides of my body until they mingle with the skeleton flowers at my hips. Continuing the effect, the gown splits at my thighs, leaving the rest of my legs bare. Nothing but a great train of feathers and flowers sweeping the floor behind me.

Just as she did with my arms, Belinda dusts my bare legs all over with so much shimmer it looks like a million diamond shavings. She leaves my feet naked.

Then, she steps back to take stock of her work. "It'll do." She drags a hand through her short tufts of hair, then curses when realizing she's smeared white paint into the dark strands.

"Why do you stay if you hate it?" I ask as she cleans up her table.

Belinda rolls her eyes. "What are you talking about? I love it!"

Turning away, Belinda bends to pick up a fallen bottle, unashamed of how her short skirt exposes her plump but well-shaped legs. Her pillowy figure is attractive, and I'm surprised she isn't on one of these levels for another reason.

When I ask, she pops up, her ample breasts jiggling beneath the tight shirt she wears. "Well, I'm no Swan, but thanks all the same. I'm a Syndicate daughter. I could have been a display, but I chose money over fame. It keeps my shoe house well stocked." She gestures to the elaborate platforms she wears. The ones with gold filigree coiling all the way up past her knees.

"Are you my preparer?"

"For tonight, yes. Don't know if I'll be back. Depends on my schedule, but if Director Force likes the finished product, then maybe. Pleasure, Swan."

Instead of shaking my hand that is still damp from paint and shimmer, Belinda leans over and plants a light kiss on my forehead, tapping it once like giving a green light to launch a product.

"By the way, you can call me Lindy."

I hope Lindy prepares me again.

OUR FAMILIAR PATTERN EMERGES. JUST as always.

Luc waits for me on the lower level, eyes marveling as I make my way down the winding staircase, careful not to get my train stuck between the railings. At first, I was confused why he didn't meet me in the bedroom suite, but the reason is obvious. Sky's up there, too.

Luc takes my hand and leans toward me, mouth aimed for my cheek.

I pull away, warning, "You know better than that."

Pausing, Luc refuses to retreat, unwilling to give up that easily. "We both know what you wanted that night."

"It doesn't matter what my body *wanted*, Luc."

"What you still want," he corrects, pressing his thumb to my chin.

My lips part from the action, and he smirks.

I narrow my eyes. "You cheated, and you know it."

"Because my brother fights so fairly." Luc rolls his words in a sarcastic coating, dropping his hand.

"It's not a competition."

He lowers his lethal brows. "The hell it isn't."

I step forward, insistent. "I've made my choice. It's not just a feeling, Luc. It's a promise. It's something you'll never understand because you only commit to something as long as it serves your purpose."

"Serenity—" he tries to interrupt.

45

I hold up a hand. "No. Wanting something is different than *knowing* something. I know I want you. Anyone can see that. Some people have a chemistry, but that's all it is. I know I want Sky, but more than that, I know I *love* him. I know I need him. Most of all, I know we're *right* for each other. It's that simple."

"You won't let me try?" His voice borders on desperate as he lifts his hand toward me. "No chance to prove you wrong?"

Shrinking, I huff, "*You* proved me wrong that night. Sky's been proving me right since he first picked me up the day I was born."

Sighing, Luc draws a hand through his hair before reaching out to cup my cheek. "I never had a chance, did I?"

"Yes, you did. I'll always respect you for what you did with the graphickers, Gull's abuser, and for giving up the Aviary. But all this—" Tracing a circle around my body, I finish, "—is work and nothing more. I hope you can respect that like I respect you."

"You expect me to come this close to you, see you become my vision, but never act on my own wishes?"

"Yes." I nod, stating the obvious. "After all, I'm just your Swan, Luc. Not your Serenity. I'm one of your Birds. I'm not asking for friendship. I'm just asking you to treat me like a human being."

"You take impossible to a new level."

"That she does!" Neil closes the door behind him.

I didn't even hear him enter, but I smile as he makes his debut, hands folded behind his back. Some of his body language reminds me of Force with how he's hunched over a little, observing my costume.

"Absolutely enchanting, sister." Neil snatches up my hand, then rubs his lips across the back of it.

"Not so bad yourself," I comment, referring to his three-piece suit.

He kisses my cheek. "We all know I clean up nicely. Same goes for him." He points to Luc. "Uh…strike that, he's always clean. Anyway, I'll be escorting you with Luc to the exhibit tonight. Daddy will bring you to the interaction."

"I thought it wasn't until midnight."

"You will have a new preparation for the interaction," Luc answers. "But the vision is not mine. All according to your father's work and design."

Neil takes my elbow, motioning to the door. "Best not to keep him waiting. Time for your grand Face of the Temple debut."

Oh joy.

SOME WARPED SENSE OF GRATITUDE emerges at the sight of a water exhibit. My father has seen to it my entrance is indeed grand. For the first time, the audience isn't behind glass but sitting in chairs. Rather, they are standing with a round of applause as I make my way down the staircase into the crowd's center. Right now, my butterflies strike poses like proud peacocks. Ugh, even they are turning bird on me. Whatever. Lightning still crackles on the edges of my Lepidoptera wings. Through all this, I keep my head raised high.

After I've ascended the small staircase that leads me to the tank's edge, the exhibit room lights all dim. Luc and Neil help me into a canoe awaiting me on the surface. Whether my father prefers me to sit or lay down is unclear, so I opt for something halfway in between by leaning against the side of the canoe and slipping one hand into the water. Luc gathers the generous train, then drapes it into the water before he and Neil send the canoe off.

Now, the lights go black while a lone spotlight bathes the canoe. Music plays in the background, notes high, melodic, and eerie. Different from the Aviary's music, but everything seems like the same old tune. I wonder when Force wants me underwater. There will be some sort of signal, I imagine, but for now, I'll play along.

First, I pulse my hand through the water, creating small ripples—something simple to start with. I rise ever so slightly, bringing my hand up so droplets follow gravity's path through the air and back to the water. Cupping the water in both hands, I toss it into the air above me, tilting so droplets tumble onto my hair. I hear nothing from the audience. Silence is required during the performance, so it's no surprise.

Suddenly, I feel water from beneath me. Not shocked at all, I want to shake my head and chuckle. *Well played, Luc.* Instead, I recline into water as the canoe begins to sink. Silly of me not to

47

notice the gaping holes inside the wood. Spreading my arms to the sides, I welcome the liquid. It's the first time I've had a train that hasn't fallen apart, but the feathers and flowers are fortunately light enough for me to bring the train along.

Taking one deep breath, I sink beneath the surface, keeping my eyes open. Tank lights swarm to life, marinating me in a rich glow—rich enough I can tell the audience has come with me. Some sort of mechanized chairs that shift downward like an amusement park ride that descends one level so they may watch my underwater performance from beyond the tank.

What I do first is plow right through the water to the glass until I can fan my hands along it. Water twirls my train all around me, and I play with it before coming up with an idea. Holding its end in my fingers, I spin my body in a circle. The white train follows. I take my dance into an arc, releasing a few breathy bubbles upon my flip. Continuing my underwater dance, I pirouette and swim in circles until I register I'm losing my buoyancy. The perfect time to dive. Curious as to how deep the tank is, I plunge straight down, more bubbles escaping, which only helps to propel me downward again. Once I reach the bottom, I push off with all my strength and course through the liquid, arms straight at my sides until I surface, gasping for air.

Music still plays in the background, and I understand why. This is the Temple. Expectations are higher. So, I breathe, then sink again. Now, I prove I can swim from one end of the tank to the other with no breaths taken. However many minutes it's been, I can't tell. As usual, this is my domain. To me, the audience doesn't exist. Down here, it's just the water and me. This is the closest nibble of freedom I get. Water is my air. Pity I can't trade my lungs for gills.

A vibration pulses its way into me. Suddenly, I realize the water at my feet has begun to froth. Bubbles grow, forming the shape of a tornado. Steeling myself, I arch my neck, holding my breath as the tornado grows to envelop me. Inside the eye of the watery twister, I close my eyes, extend my arms, and play to the sensational dance as my train twirls to the rhythm. The feathers and flowers weave all around my body just to spin out again until the tornado propels me higher, rocketing my body up and up and up until…

I breathe air, flipping my hair as most of my body is launched out of the water, flying for three brief moments until I fall to a musical encore of screaming trumpets and bellowing drums.

Finally, I float on my back for the finale, breathless, sweeping my arms as if I'm forming a water angel. One last held note, and the lights darken. Fatigued but not yet drained, I swim for the edge of the tank where Luc and Neil help me out of the water. I lean on my brother for support, pausing to rest my forehead on his shoulder.

"You won't believe the sprite lights I got from that," Neil murmurs in my ear above the standing ovation, which is like thunder in the room. "By the weekend, these will be on every magazine cover in the world. You're going global, sis. Congratulations."

"Thrilled, Neil," I quip. "Just thrilled."

Ten

TolerAnce

Bliss

OUR FATHER ARRANGED A PRIVATE box for us for Serenity's open-ing night. She will have many more to come whether she re-alizes it or not. He has high expectations and demands they be met. She won't have much rest unlike the Aviary. I can't possibly predict the number of interactions since that is a cost factor or a business-related one. Sometimes, in the interest of diplomacy or corporate connections, Force will arrange for complimentary ses-sions to sweeten or sometimes proffer a business deal, merger, or contract—any number of things. Up till this point, the sessions have been private ones fulfilled by me.

Now, there will be interactions featuring us both. Perhaps I never expected he would find her. He always said I doubted him. Another reason for his changing my name. At least Serenity and I have one thing in common—neither of us will ever doubt him again.

She is the Swan incarnate. Having seen no other roles, I still know this will always be her best one. Like our father, Serenity wears all her emotions so loosely. At any point, she can multiply them, breeding expressions faster than rabbits. Her face doesn't express her namesake; it expresses mine.

I wonder how well she will perform with the other exhibits my father has in mind.

I can adopt any pose, fit myself into any skin, and open my-self up like a nesting doll to a client while keeping them always wanting more, always yearning to open another and another until they come to the last one. What they never understand is they will never find it. It's so microscopic, it can't be seen or even touched. Like bacteria.

Despite this, I don't know what to make of this new interaction. In fact, it turns my insides to rot.

Why can I stomach the thought of a thousand more nights spent with a dozen or more men… but not one interaction with my own sister?

"Come, Mara." Force leans over in the box to announce, "I will return you to your room where Serenity will join us. You will spend the next couple of hours with her before the interaction preparations. I have a feeling this encounter will be rather difficult, and I trust you to see to it she's ready."

"Yes, Father."

"And Mara…" Pausing, he sweeps a few of my dark curls over my shoulder before finishing, "Immediately after your encounter, we will commence Serenity's training. If all goes well, this may be the night I finally address you by your born name."

It all comes down to Serenity, then.

Once we reach my bedroom, Director Aldaine and Neil are standing there with Serenity, who is still dressed in her Swan/Skeleton Flower ensemble, a veritable creek in the wake of the soaked train.

Force nods to both young men before approaching Serenity with outstretched arms. "Well done, daughter."

He wastes no time before embracing her. I would smile. I would lean into the strength of his stance. I would breathe in his familiar cologne. Love the brush of his stubble against my soft cheek. Serenity does none of these things. She reacts like he's a sparkler, almost jumping back to avoid catching fiery sparks from hitting her. As always, our father pursues until he gets what he wants. She squirms and cringes through it all before he finally releases her to address Director Aldaine.

"Excellent transformation, Luc."

It's the first time I've heard the director's name. It suits him well. I appreciate the simple roll of the tongue it affords.

"Mara will help you undress," Father tells Serenity. "I look forward to your interaction later tonight."

He kisses her cheek and departs. Luc's eyes stray from her once when I advance toward the three of them. However, it's the first time they linger. In the Breakable Room, there was a momentary glance. This is more. He takes in the white dress my father selected for me this evening. He takes in the way it accentuates my curves, leaving little to the imagination. It's an observance I've come to recognize so well. Second nature for men. Or perhaps… first nature.

I walk past them, then open the door to my room. "Only Serenity, please," I request, and they both eye her.

"Great performance," Neil mentions with a wink before turning around.

Luc seems like he wants to do more, but there is a hardness to Serenity's eyes. She's sharpened them with a diamond durability. He nods to her, glances at me once more, and then turns the corner to the adjoining hallway.

I decide to opt for a diversion topic to keep our conversation off our nonexistent relationship. "I saw your finale performance at the Aviary. The first time a director has become part of an exhibit. But it seems much has changed since then." I close the door once the rest of her train is free.

"That's an understatement," she drawls.

"Come to my vanity. I'll help you out of your dress."

"Lindy sealed on the feathers. How will you—?"

"I have the remover. I know what to do." Such a simple task. I could do it in my sleep.

"I hope you'll teach me sometime. I'd like to remove my own costumes."

Of course she would. I don't offer her any acknowledgement because I have no interest in teaching her any of the things I know. As it is, my father's request to keep her stable for the interaction seems mountainous.

When I sit her in front of the vanity, I decide a simple revelation will suffice. "Tonight's interaction will be nyotaimori."

Stunned, she shakes her head, damp hair whipping in the process. "How do you know what it's going to be? And nyo-what?"

I hand her a robe, so she can use it to cover herself when the time comes.

52

"I am Yin."

I give her the obvious reason as I start to work on her costume, detaching the lower part of the gown and then removing the feathers at her hips, moving upward. The sight of the familiar birthmark on her thigh—a replica to mine—does not escape my notice.

"I am the dark one who knows secrets and mysteries. It's not for Yang. Yang is too unpredictable. Yang belongs to passion."

"Isn't Yang originally masculine?"

I can't help but smirk a little at how she so easily deviates from the overarching interaction subject.

"Yes, but we both know you are more masculine. More like our father than any of his children." I've reached her navel area now. My hands work quickly but effectively as they always do.

"So, what is this interaction?"

"Nyotaimori is translated as female body arrangement. It can be any food, really, but the most common is sushi. Its roots are Japanese."

"You've done it before?"

"Dressed in my own skin, yes. Not as Yin."

I peel apart more feathers. Her skin is softer than mine, but when my fingers touch the center of her chest between her cleavage, she winces.

"Did I—"

"No…" She rushes to speak as if trying to assuage any guilt even though I don't feel any. "I had cuts there just a couple of months ago. It's difficult to forget."

"Memories are powerful things." I remember everything.

"What happens during the interaction?" she questions.

"Our artisan will prepare us as the Yin and Yang, we will take our places on the tables, and food preparers will arrange the delicacies on our bodies, then the clients will come forward to sup."

"Is that all?"

"Well, as stated in the prior arrangement, they will be permitted to touch me, but they will only touch your food. And any continued session will be completed by me, but I doubt that will be the case tonight. Our father wants to commence your training immediately."

I peel off the last feather on her breast, and she doesn't delay in covering herself with the robe.

"Why did you do it?"

"Do what?" I wonder.

"You know what I'm talking about. In the Breakable Room."

"I don't know." I work the remover into the feathers at her neck, using a tool to skin them, ignoring her cringe when I rip just a little. Not enough remover.

"Yes, you do. You've been spending weeks with her. No one who meets her can help it. Our mother is the most lovable person on earth, Bliss. And considering the man you've spent your life with is the easiest person to hate—"

"I don't hate him," I deny.

"I wasn't saying anything about your feelings. Just who he is. Something about him makes people want to hate him."

"Not for me." I look up. "And you're wrong. He couldn't have risen to such a height living off the hate of others."

"True," she agrees. "He has to feel fear. Fear and hate are both immensely powerful."

"So is respect."

"You don't respect him."

"I have a healthy obedience." Turning my eyes back to her skin, I keep them there. "A tolerance because I understand him."

"Is that what you have for me?" she asks once I reach the upper edge of her throat. "Tolerance?"

"You're very perceptive, Serenity."

"I want it to be more."

"I know." I still don't look at her.

"Do you think we'll ever be—"

"No."

I finish with the last feather. The floor drowns from their weight. Now, the train looks more like one soggy white mess. Serenity doesn't stand from the chair. She's curled into herself a little. I don't know why she's so shy. I've seen her body before. I see it in the mirror every single day.

"Our artisan will be here in another hour to prepare us."

"You don't call her a preparer?"

"No." I shake my head. "On this level of the Penthouse, they are no longer preparers. They are artisans because they are so skilled at what they do that they only prepare one person. Except for tonight. For the first time in years, he will have one more."

Serenity looks like she's about to leap from the chair. "He?"

"He," I resound.

Eleven

YiN andYaNg

SERENITY

"DON'T COME NEAR ME," I warn the young man when he enters Bliss's bedroom with a carrying case of items at his side.

I back up against the vanity. A male preparer. How could my father ever think—? How could Bliss ever—?

He scrutinizes me, head tilting in a curious manner, dark ginger locks of his hair falling over his brow he doesn't concern himself with. The ends of his short ponytail graze the edge of his neck just beneath his ear when he tips his face toward me. All Bliss does is smile when he sets his carrying case next to the vanity without saying a word. His next move stuns me; he kneels, bowing his head and opening his hand, palm up. Inside is a delicate paper swan. Beak thinned and folded to a perfect point, tail nothing more than a tiny, white triangle, neck curved and lower body straight as the bottom of a child's paper boat.

"Queran doesn't speak much," Bliss says, removing her outer robe and hanging it on a hook. "He prefers to communicate through those. Occasionally, we'll get a few words out of him."

I stare at the young man as he presents me with the welcoming token. My fingers tremble as I accept, tips just brushing the swan head. He rises, reaches a hand to me, and then touches one of his thumbs to my left eye before gesturing to Bliss, beckoning me to watch.

Remaining rooted to my spot against the wall, I observe as he sways to Bliss's side. His body is tall and lanky but with just a hint of graceful muscles—almost like a dancer's. Then, he removes the

56

gold chain around her neck, places it on the vanity, and follows suit with her lingerie until she is a naked canvas glancing back at her shell in the mirror. Her gaze doesn't hold her reflection long.

The only thing he won't have to change is her hair since she has a permanent implant, which changed it dark long ago from what I've learned. Next, Queran mixes a color palette of whites—subtle ivory, frost with a hint of shimmer blue, chiffon, cream betraying a honey glow, and coconuts with an under layer of pink. For the next few minutes, I study him as he blends all these onto her face with hands of soft and skilled expertise. Sweeping, curving, accenting, even swirling—all his paintbrushes perform synchronized dances along my sister's skin. Not once do his eyes drift to places I consider "special". Not once does he inhale quickly, betraying any lust. Every now and then, I catch him biting on his lower lip, but he never licks them. Nor do I ever detect anything other than his pale eggshell cheeks. They never crack to let a flush swell.

There's something so wrong about him... but so right for the Faces of the Temple that must be preserved—never touched by an artisan.

Bliss reveals the answer to Queran's puzzle.

"Queran was selected especially by our father for the Penthouse. He was born with a lower sex drive, which can happen in some men, and he was apprenticed to a Temple artisan when he was a child."

She smiles at him as he drapes a towel over his arm and removes the white bowls of paint from his workstation.

"He mastered his craft even before his superior did," Bliss says. "They called him a prodigy. And he decided to stay past his adolescence. But artisans operating on a higher level who choose a Temple career must take an oath and then undergo the operation."

"Operation?" I thread my hands together at my upper thighs where the silk robe Bliss has given me ends. Then, I squeeze my arms into my body.

"Not surgical. Chemical. I shudder when I think of the brutal cutting methods people used before our medical advances. Here, they have a different method where they inject a permanent chemical implant that stunts the sex drive and lowers testosterone."

I rub a hand up and down my arm. "Why do they bother? Security guards even use the girls' services."

"The lower-level preparers don't have such procedures. But the relationship between girl and artisan is remarkably close in the Penthouse. An artisan remains with her for years. There must be absolute—"

"Trust?" No, I shake my head. That doesn't fit. Bliss doesn't strike me as the kind of person who cares about trust.

"Control," she corrects. "It's essential when you have someone touching your body every day. Where security is stationed, there are cameras, and they are also physically monitored during their guard hours, but monitors are removed after those hours are over. But on this level, artisans…require more."

Bliss stands, and Queran motions to the glass chamber I first noticed when we entered the preparation room. The artisan opens the door for her, and she steps inside. He closes it after her. I don't look away when warm, golden orbs bathe her in a soft glow. That's when I realize it's a drying chamber so the first layer of paint may dry more effectively. It only takes a minute or two before she is finished, and he opens the door. Queran doesn't even need to guide her. This is routine for my sister—something she's not only practiced at but excels.

After she sits, Queran sweeps dramatic black across Bliss's skin until there is nothing left but the never-ending circle of white just around her eyes and from the pure ghost inside the contact lenses she wears. He even paints her eyelashes white to enhance the eye's pure power. Final stroke is to release her hair, which he straightens before coiling it into a tight, thick bun on the top of her head. He doesn't even need to harness any recalcitrant strands; her hair is more obedient than mine.

She turns around to present herself. Yin. The whites of her eyes are the good in the evil. If only I could spread that white— mushroom it until it sucks up all the black of what has been done to her. If only we could find our balance inside each other just as easily as it's painted on the outside. I must hope, no, *believe* it can happen.

I start to breathe heavier because it's my turn, and Queran gestures to the chair. Curling my hands to my throat, pressing on the skin there, I try to remember why I am doing this. The image of my mother dressed as the Unicorn seizes my blood, electrifying tiny lightning storms to burn my arteries. Exactly what my heart needs. But when I stand before the vanity—despite knowing what Queran is—or rather what he is *not*—my body doesn't stop trembling. I bite my lip to suppress a gasp when he eases my hair to my back, then opens the robe straps and slides it down the curves of my shoulders. Loose enough that just after I've blinked, the robe has pooled to my feet. Chilly air wraps around all my skin, and I find myself shivering. Queran lights his hands on my underwear, but I need a moment. I rush to sit on the chair first, then curl my body into a ball, hands gripping my legs, digging my knees into my chest.

This place isn't like the Garden or Aviary where my display was safely tucked behind glass—a spectacle but not an interaction as I'm about to share with Bliss. Even if she says I will be untouchable, another man will touch me now.

Resting my forehead on my knees, I whimper just a little.

Maybe If Bliss and I were similar, this would be better. Maybe if she wasn't really my Yin, I could cope. But we have nothing in common.

Our mother. We have our mother in common.

Queran touches me. I'd hoped Bliss would touch me first, cup my shoulder, pat my head—some outward show of consolation—but she still stands in the center of the room. Not preoccupied but not concerned either. Nor curious. Just studying me with a blank expression on her face, one that almost registers confusion. On the contrary, Queran tilts my chin up to his eyes, which are so young I could fool myself into believing they are a child's eyes. I suppose he is beautiful in his own way with his deep-set eyes the color of blue salt—almost electric. Not like Luc's, which are steel ships cutting through sea, but Queran's are the most animated part of him. His dark spiced pony accents his eyes even more. Skin an unordinary shade of pale spent from so much time in these cold walls. I'm sure he sees little of the outside.

"Shh…sweet girl." His voice is low, caught halfway between a murmur and a whisper.

His breath is clean, as sterile as these skyscraper walls.

He picks up a piece of paper nearby, takes his time to arrange it into a diamond shape before folding the points in, expertly curving the inner edge to create a dipping V that becomes a paper heart. After he presses it to my nude chest, he points to the delicate center. Then, he brings it to his lips and whispers another 'shh' before kissing it and cupping the origami inside his hands like he's holding a tender bundle of stardust. I receive the message. Inside is what matters. He just paints the outside, but he will care for what's outside just as much as he cares about what's inside.

Finally, Queran picks up the white spray and sweeps it up and down my body. I bite my lower lip, pressing my eyes together before nodding in surrender. Then, he raises one finger, sets the sprayer down, and grabs a few of his paintbrushes. A moment later, Queran assumes all my hair and raises it above my neck, then sticks the paintbrushes in to maintain its position. I recognize it as his way of lending a small piece of himself to me. It's enough, but—

"I-I might still need some time," I croak out. "In between. Um…" I stare at his puzzled expression and try to clarify, summoning the word I'm searching for. "Breaks?"

Judging from his smile, I take it as a sign he can work with me on that. I start to lower my knees, but he touches both and motions for me to remain put. After which he sets to work on my face, applying a sealer, traveling from there to my throat, upper chest, and moving down my arms first. Then, he uses the sprayer, which paints a winter landscape on my skin. He sprinkles shimmer, dusting it everywhere paint is until I can imagine my limbs are like those crystallized tree branches one sees on an early winter morning after a light snowfall.

Queran picks up a brush, then sweeps it toward my breast. Inhaling, I hold up a hand to signal a break. I close my eyes. Count my breaths. Inhale, exhale, inhale. Why this is so difficult? Maybe because the interaction is coming. Am I trying in vain to delay it? Or is it really because of Queran? I drag my legs up to flatten my knees against my breasts before daring myself to look him in the eye. No scorn, impatience, or even amusement at my expense. No, his expression is more pensive. Not curious but thoughtful. At first, I think I notice one eye twitch and a muscle tighten in his jaw, but it must be a trick of the lights because he clears his throat, nods, and raises one finger before walking away.

I watch as he calmly strides to the bathroom door.

Bliss giggles just a little from behind me. "No, Serenity, he might be a eunuch, but the urination urge is not suppressed."

Oh.

A black Yin vision, Bliss sways toward me, not one iota of her skin out of place. Her eyes are like stars in a pitch-black sky. She scoots into the chair next to me and leans to the side, expression almost bewildered.

"Why are you insecure?"

"I'm not," I snap, a little too harshly. "I just…don't like people touching me. This body is mine, and I don't like someone else's hands, especially another man's—"

"It's just a brush."

"Someone's eyes, then."

"But you've performed as the Swan and the Skeleton Flower. How could eyes possibly bother you?"

"It makes me sick every time, wondering what they are thinking, what they *feel* when they look at me."

"Don't let it. It doesn't matter," Bliss states, manner all definitions of simple. "Especially with Queran."

I flick my head toward her, eyes callous. "Doesn't it matter what I *feel*?"

She shakes her head. Just once. But firmly. "No, it doesn't."

I don't get the chance to ask her what she feels because Queran emerges from the bathroom. Some part of me feels more relaxed now. Amazing how such a simple, human act like the need to urinate can put me more at ease. So, I drop my knees and bare my breasts to him. What helps is how his expert hand never once touches me. No rubbing of knuckles even as he leans in to swirl extra white paint and shimmer around each of my nipples. No brushing of the base of his palm when he wisps the brush upward. His eyes harness my skin, concentrated on the winter landscape. I almost feel like one of his origami shapes. Folding Serenity over and over to create some new entity.

Yang.

I stare at her now with her lashes dark and mesmerizing to

convey the black pearl irises, so dark I can't even detect my pupils. Once I'm under the heated glow of lights and warm fans that arrange for the paint to dry, it's much more comforting. Queran doesn't look at me. Or Bliss for that matter. Queran silently goes about his tasks, cleaning up his workstation and placing things back in their proper places, but he does toss away the bowls even though they have some paint left in them. He also drops the paint-brushes into the trash bucket.

"Queran never uses the same brush twice," Bliss informs me. "It's his way of showing respect."

Steeling my shoulders, I turn to face my sister. "What now?"

"Now, we take the elevator to the enclosed observation deck. Our tables will be there, and then Queran, along with food pre-parers, will begin the next stage."

BLISS IS SO MUCH BETTER at this than me. Trained her entire life under our father's parasitic care, she closes her eyes and remains perfectly still. Tree roots have grown out of her back, fusing her skin to the table. The flat surface is long enough to accommodate both our bodies, but it's shaped like the Yin-Yang symbol. Our heads positioned just next to each other, but her body pointed in one direction and mine in the opposite. Her head is directed at the moon, but mine is lined up with the east where the rising sun never sleeps—only shifts to another part of the world. Everything is staged down to the very last detail. No room for error.

With our combined body warmth, Queran and the others need to move more quickly to prevent the food from growing warm from the heat of our flesh. All cold sushi, of course, but I learn there will be an intermission followed by cold desserts. As the observation deck is enclosed, the environment is air condi-tioned to help preserve the experience. It's too cold. I wonder if the glass windows overlooking the expansive Boroughs and be-yond will frost over.

Just as Queran places two lone Skeleton Flowers across each of my painted nipples and nothing else, I begin to chase my breath. Bliss is more covered. Sushi rolls wrapped in deep seaweed-green casings that blend in with the color of her skin decorate her breasts.

Yang is more exposed than Yin. Yin is winter and secrets. Yang is summer and passion.

Closing my eyes, I harness the image of my mother and inhale deeply. Slowly. If I can't do this, Force will whip her. If I can't do this, he will punish her in my place. I steel myself. My body is a dragon, my breath is its smoke. In another moment or two, I manage to slow my heartbeat so my chest doesn't heave so much. Queran replaces the Skeleton Flowers.

"How can you—" I start to ask Bliss, but my voice sounds raspy. Need water. My vocal chords have turned to dried lint.

"I was born with an X chromosome," Bliss responds, picking up on my question, her chest as even as a ripple in a pond. "From the womb, I was destined as a sexual entity. If people view me as that no matter what I do, then I may as well use it to my advantage. Experiences like this are a treat."

I can almost hear my father's voice lacing her vocal chords.

Out of the corner of my eye, I watch as Queran adds another sushi roll to the allotment around Bliss's navel. Black and dark green casings for her, white-themed sushi items for me. Goose bumps parade on my skin as he forms delicate sushi patterns leading down to my pelvis before he assembles more Skeleton Flowers there to shroud my private area. Despite knowing what Queran is, I still can't help my eyes drifting to his lower regions. Stiller than a broken train. No tenseness in his body, just hyper-awareness dictated by how his eyes settle upon mine just after he finishes.

"Shh, sweet girl."

He touches two fingers to my lips to calm the seismic activity causing them to tremble. Then, he brushes the backs of his knuckles across my cheek, quashing a tear. Queran offers me no comforting words unlike Dove. Magnolia's blindness was its own comfort. Lindy's frantic, fast hands trying to keep up with her words were another. To me, the most comforting thing about Queran is his origami—his paper shapes that speak for him. I picture the way his subtle fingers work the paper into a precise fold when his cool breath sinks onto my forehead so he may kiss my brow.

I wish the floor could become a sink hole. For a moment, I imagine the table under us turning to wispy clouds and the chrome and glass floor melting into a silver waterfall for Bliss and me to slide all the way down the Temple and out through the front doors so we can walk away and never turn back.

"You must learn to indulge in these sorts of experiences," Bliss says without glancing at me once. "There is more *appreciation* involved. They are sensual and artistic. The female form is something to be admired and celebrated. The experience of nyotaimori is far more delicate than most encounters here."

"It doesn't seem delicate to me."

"I've had training. You haven't," she says. "That is what make us the fire and ice, the Yin and Yang of the Temple. I carry the secrets and belong to the night. You have fire and your beautiful virginity. This balance grants our clients a fuller, more meaningful fantasy. "

That's why Queran has enhanced my curls by tinting them with a shimmer to bring out my inner Yang.

Suddenly, I want him back. I want him to leave me with one last paper object to get me through this. As soon as he closes the door and men begin to enter the room after him, I start to gasp again. I hadn't expected this many. Twenty in all. They are here for a feast. And we are the vessels. They wear business suits, black. But one by one, they remove their suit coats, a few draping them over their chairs and others much less concerned when they take in the display. *Our* display. About half are young. In their thirties, I'd wager. Others, it's difficult to tell. And the seniors of the group are well into their fifties. Like Force. Not one makes a move toward the food. Their eyes taste us, drift across our sensual areas, eager and ready.

Then, our father enters. Naturally, he would enter from a higher location—a balcony that oversees the interaction. Without addressing his guests, Force places his hands on the railing and pauses to study his daughters. He nods approvingly. At last, after that moment has practically circumnavigated the globe, Force extends a hand and welcomes the men.

"My esteemed guests, I thank you for joining me on this momentous occasion and sharing in this singular tradition. On this night, I am pleased to grant to you—my highest shareholders—the grand opening of the Temple Faces Interaction. As you well know..." Chuckling, he gestures to the table. "The treasures that lie before you are identical twins, but I'll wager you can tell them apart."

All the men around us laugh. Considering my Swan debut earlier, of course they know who is who. Even if they were given no information prior, they know who is Yin and who is Yang. They know who the long-lost Temple daughter is. The one my father is finally unearthing and bringing to light while Bliss will always remain in the shadows, behind the scenes.

"After all these years, your keen-sense business minds and eyes may finally savor the sight of more than one twin. My daughters. My prized possession."

He states the last word in singular tense. Not plural.

"I welcome you to enjoy the meal but to respect the vessels who serve it. Pay homage to my miracle. Feed on their beauty for one night. And understand how high I hold your regard and your support and positions in my company. Thank you for your time and attention, gentlemen. You may now eat."

Force remains where he is as the meal commences.

It's clear everyone here knows the legend of the missing twin because their eyes circle my body like vultures. More so than Bliss's. When I notice one man lean over to pluck a sushi roll with his chopsticks from my sister's breast, my intestines tighten up, the butterflies in my belly protesting, reaching for their invisible war hammers. What surprises me the most is how she remains perfectly still without moving or opening her eyes. I can't think about her one more moment when a set of lips rubs the line of her cleavage to snatch up a black sushi roll from the long banana leaves. However, I know my father must have given these men some prior information. Perhaps even a contract in writing because no skin touches mine—lips, hands, or otherwise.

Two men smile down at me. Not affectionately. Not at all. Despite the boundaries, they find other methods. Like teasing their chopsticks onto the rolls at my legs, just above my thighs. Chopsticks linger, rubbing my skin sensitively, rousing my breath and body, testing me. Laughter rolls about the room, men's voices tripping over each other's, but I catch a few familiar words like 'the Swan,' and 'Skeleton Flower,' and 'Force has outdone himself this time'.

One man reaches up, hand eager for my hair.

"You know the rules, Tristan," another warns him.

I pause to glance up at my father, who apparently couldn't care less about Bliss. His eyes are only for me, and they are keenly aware of the man on my left.

Twisting my head to Tristan, I turn my eyes into two black predators.

"Careful," the man next to him warns, elbowing his arm. "Yang is the fierce one."

"I'd take hell itself if I could get her in my bed."

"Rumor is he's welcoming suitors of all levels, but he's letting her choose her own mate."

Tristan grins at me. "Lucky bastard."

"Not so lucky. She'll still retain ownership. Pot of gold still in her name."

"Beautiful name."

I bite hard on my lower lip, particularly when I feel a chopstick toying with one of the skeleton flowers over my nipple.

"I think I'll risk the wrath of hell for one kiss."

Too distracted from the other greedy chopsticks, I register Tristan's words right before the immediate shock of him kissing me, sinking his tongue past my lips in the same moment. It's not the first time I've been kissed against my will, but each time it happens, it's different. Like having a brush with death. He should've been prepared for hell because I draw blood when I bite down on his tongue. He leaps back, releasing a slight yelp, and I turn to the balcony and smile at my father, whose expression is triumphant when Tristan's chair ends up doubling over from the inertia of his action.

"You said hell itself," Tristan's friend reminds him.

A dethroned Tristan touches a finger to his mouth and winks at me. "Hell never tasted so sweet."

That one moment of power and tiny drop of blood I can still taste in my mouth grants me the power I need to get through this. The men rush too much, all greedy hands and fingers and lusting eyes. One even suggests using the chopsticks to work away at the pasted Skeleton Flowers, but one brazen gaze from me and another reminder to respect the vessel of Yang, not to mention Tristan's wounded tongue, keeps them at a safe distance. Well, not really *safe*. Safe would be Antarctica. But safe enough from violence.

They compensate with Bliss. She takes it all. Sucks down every drop of their lust without moving at all.

My sister astounds me.

BLISS

YANG'S BIT OF OUTBURST MAKES it harder for me to concentrate, but I still perform without flinching. I know just how to lie still. Knees bent slightly, legs open and rotated out to the sides at a one-hundred-and-eighty-degree angle, unlike Yang who keeps her body sealed tighter than a clam shell. What the men do to my body gives me no reason to flinch. Over the years, I've learned to drown out the sensations. Fingers, hands, lips… they all land but do not strike. To me, they are invisible. Not to Yang. That is who she is to me in this moment. Serenity does not exist just as Bliss and Mara do not exist—only Yin.

Overhearing the yelp of the man off to her side, I almost want to turn my head to discover the source, but I listen to their conversation instead for answers. No touching was specified, but I hadn't believed she'd bite him. I hope she'll be ready for another round after the intermission is over.

These men will still manage to fit more into their stomach after gorging themselves on a banquet of sushi. After all, their appetites are impossible to satisfy. For now, they empty the room to enjoy dessert cocktails served on the adjoining terrace. Mechanized blinds are lowered to give the preparers more privacy.

Queran approaches Serenity first, but she doesn't give him the chance to begin preparing her for the dessert round. Instead, she rises, slides off the table, her bare feet smacking the floor before turning toward the stairs. Judging from the determination in her eyes, I know she's about to ascend the stairs to the balcony and confront our father. That would be a mistake.

Careless of the banana leaves sliding off my body, I leap off the table to catch up to her. Grabbing her arm, I halt her from her pursuit and glance up briefly to see our father nod at me, gesturing his confirmation of my act.

"Serenity." I choose to address her by her real name in this instance. "You need to take your place again."

"I'm not some damn piece of pleasure meat!" She takes her arm back, then shoves me away.

"Don't forget you agreed to this," I stab at her, reminding her of our bargain.

"You know what's worse than having their eyes so close and their breath all over my skin?" She pauses before doing her best to jab me with her own intense gaze. "Seeing their hands all over you but watching the way you stomach it all."

The way she scrutinizes me now, so full of disappointment, it's the way Force has watched me every day since I can remember. Years ago, I gave up trying to change it and accepted what I was. I can only please to a point. They'll always want more. But Serenity wants more in a different way, but my Yin path was forged at birth. There is no other course.

She's making it harder on herself—expecting more where there is less. I can be her guide, her mentor, but I can never be her friend. Nor will I ever be a sister. After tonight, she will understand that. After Father commences her training and she rains down her first scar on my back, she will understand it's the point of no return for us.

One never forgets the first time.

Father never has.

Neither will I.

Twelve

ThE UltiMate PoWer

SERENITY

OESN'T SHE UNDERSTAND THIS INTERACTION is gutting me twice over? Whether or not they touch me, I still feel it every time they touch her. Because every curve is the same. When their unknowing fingers slide across our shared birthmark, I sense it on my own thigh. Nothing inside is the same, but our bodies are mirrors pointed at one another. Doesn't that count for anything? I need something. I want something from her—something I can hold onto for us both because this interaction will never be just about me.

"Tell me you love her, Bliss. Please. I can get through this if you just tell me you love her."

Bliss sighs, black arms placated in front of her, one white eye focused on me. "You said it yourself. Serafina is the easiest person in the world to love."

She doesn't give me exactly what I want, but it's the closest I'm going to get. It's enough. I turn back to the table where Queran is waiting. Serene smile, fanned-out hand that is calm, patient. One deep breath before I lie on the table again.

Every dessert is chilled, and it yanks more gooseflesh onto my skin. While other preparers arrange small frozen scoopfuls of green-tea ice cream onto areas of Bliss, Queran arranges chocolate-covered strawberries and dark truffles on mine. There is no time for any sort of delays. No second wasted due to the risk of melting. The preparers exit the room in record time, and the men file in and resume their seats.

69

For the most part, they behave. With me in any case. Despite the difference in dessert as opposed to sushi, they've all been instructed to use their chopsticks. I suppose I couldn't expect them to use just spoons for the ice cream, but the sight of their mouths on my sister's skin, even the sensual parts, causes me to cringe. Instead, I close my eyes and concentrate on breathing until I hear the appreciative murmur in my ear.

"Could be my imagination, but I believe your skin sweetens dessert more," Tristan tells me.

"So happy to hear."

All the men at the table pause as if my sarcastic statement has broken some cardinal rule. I notice Bliss's body tense, and I glance up to see my father frowning. I guess that means I was not supposed to talk.

However, he manages to turn my recovery into an opportunity. "What you have just witnessed, gentlemen, is Yang's forthrightness. An openness not seen in Yin. Yin remains silent and dark. For the first time in the nyotaimori experience, a vessel may choose to speak. Perhaps, you would enjoy the opportunity of asking her a question or two. Simply afford her the courtesy of a Yang title."

"Not a problem with me at all," Tristan declares, plucking up a strawberry strategically placed beneath the swell of my left breast.

"Yang," another man, who sits on the opposite side of the table, addresses me. I don't turn my head, but I listen. "How did you learn to master the art of underwater dance?"

Underwater dance? Is that what they call swimming now?

Force has no one to blame but himself. He's giving me permission to talk, so he should expect a show.

"I learned in many of the hotels my family stayed in while we were on the run from my demon father." I say it all with a smile.

A few of the men chuckle while the rest remain silent, gazes keenly aware of Force, wondering if he will whip his daughter's sharp tongue.

It's unsurprising Tristan breaks the silence, the sides of his chopsticks purposefully planted on my right nipple's skeleton flower so he may grip a truffle beside it. "Will there be any more underwater viewings in the future? If so, I will pay to come see."

70

"You'll have to ask my father." I put the words to him, training my eye on him as Tristan raises the truffle to his mouth.

Cunning fingers pinch my thigh. I wince like I've been stung. The sensation is like a sting, but it reminds me of a burn. Too much of a spark that hurts.

My father noticed the movement, too, because next, he bellows, "Guards, remove Mr. Drake from the table and escort him from Temple property." Force begins to turn aside from the balcony, making for the stairs.

Drake's brow creases from the order, but now that he's been caught, he's more than eager to try again. Whatever his business connection to my father is unclear, but when he turns to give me a knowing smirk, it's obvious he's willing to jeopardize it. His method is completely different than Tristan's daring spontaneity that was more of a show for the other men. No, Drake is doing this for himself. Far more than just fear engulfs me when he suddenly rips at one of the skeleton flowers, his hand descending.

It does not land.

In the same moment the guards haul him backward, I sit up straight, upsetting the few delectable leftovers, which topple to the floor. Doing my best not to whimper, I bring my knees up to my chest and anchor them there. Out of the corner of my eye, I see my father stand before Drake, who has succumbed to his knees from the guards' pressure.

"You will be banned from the Temple from now on," Force notifies him. "And consider our merger rescinded."

"*No.*" Drake grits his teeth. "I've invested millions in this enterprise. You cannot walk away now."

"Watch me."

Force doesn't walk away. Instead, he strides toward me, training his hand on the chair ends of his other clients while the guards yank Drake to his feet and practically drag him from the room. After circling the table until he stands in front of me, Force studies me once as if checking on me before addressing the other men.

"Please continue to enjoy the remainder of the experience with Yin. You must excuse my other daughter as she takes her leave now. At the end of the night, you will be given a complimentary pass to her next exhibit. Remember to apply on the registrar's site if you wish to purchase a backstage pass for a meeting."

My father leaves me dumbfounded when he removes his suit jacket and drapes it around my quivering shoulders before coaxing me off the table.

"Serenity, come now."

Without looking back at Bliss, I lean into my father, who wraps one arm around my shoulder and urges my head to tilt to his chest. It's much warmer than I expected it would be. His heartbeat isn't as quick as I expected either. Much slower. Because he is in control here. This is his kingdom. And I am his long-lost princess.

BLISS

I KNEW THIS WOULD HAPPEN.

Our father has a way about him. I knew it wouldn't take long for her to stop resenting the monster she's always said he is. She doesn't know how familiar his antics are. The use of a great deed to manipulate. This is a simple trick of the eyes, a conjuror's mind game. I wouldn't be surprised if he orchestrated the whole thing, planned this prior with Drake. All for her.

This is the first stage of the training process.

This is the breakdown.

Thirteen

BliSs'HeArt

SERENITY

As soon as we leave the room and embark into the hallway, the only thing I want to do is put a canyon-filled planet between my father and me, but I stay where I am instead. Force pauses to summon me.

"Serenity." He turns me to face him, then cups my chin. "I may allow any man to bask in your presence because the world should be your oyster. It should worship you. But I won't let any man hurt you in any way."

Squeamish when he starts to do up the buttons of his suit jacket to cover me, I change tactics. "*You've* hurt me."

Force's smile is contemplative. Then, he touches my cheek. "It won't take long for your mother to adopt her old routine. And it won't be for her daughters this time. It will be for herself. She can't deny who she is. None of us can."

"You left your damage inside of her. And my real father spent years picking it out."

"You still don't see, my pearl."

Force goes to touch my hair. I jerk away, but his hand still finds its way there. While winding his fingers around the nape of my neck, he leans over to murmur his breath across my face. "Your mother was born damaged. You and I were born to damage. I'll teach you how to crush whole worlds, Serenity."

It's the first time I've felt afraid of him. Because of the training? No, it's the fear he's right. All the feelings from the Shed resurface. No matter how much I want to deny it—that Jade just left some of her Venus Fly Trap claws in me—I know it's more than that. It's something that comes from deep inside me. A monster snapping at my butterflies. A monster made of lightning. A hand gripping a whip to strike.

Except this time, I won't be using it on the man I love. It will be even worse. I'll be using it on my own blood. My own reflection staring right back at me.

Force kisses my forehead, and I close my eyes.

Sky will need to kiss me raw after this just to get the smell of my father off me. I'll gladly take the smell of Sky-stuck-in-Temple-rafters-all-day over Force's cologne any time. Over the past few weeks, Sky's managed a shower here and there, but we keep them short in case of any emergency visitors. At least we've been able to spend more time with each other than we ever had in the Garden or the Aviary. Sometimes, it reminds me of the hotels we grew up in. That's what I hang onto when my father escorts me back to Bliss's bedroom where Queran will remove Yang.

INSTEAD OF REMOVING THE PAINT by hand, Queran helps me into an already-prepared bath. Smelling chemicals but also sensing warmth in the water, I slide in. He gestures for me to keep my eyes closed when I submerge. Careful, I press my eyes shut, remain under for about three minutes. When I surface, the water has turned a milky white from all the paint that has magically disappeared from my skin.

The bath is short, but Queran has a robe ready for me. Not silk, this one is fuller and breathes well. As I settle into it, I consider how it should be odd without Bliss here, but it doesn't feel like it. Based on my preparation experience with Queran as well as knowing what he is, it's simple to trust him. I almost reveal how I'd like him to teach me how to paper fold, but I don't think I could master it like he could—impatient sort that I am. Sky can attest as to how many things I've given up on because they didn't come naturally.

Not swimming.

I wonder if Bliss knows how to swim like me.

"Queran?" I study the young man in the mirror as he brushes

my hair. He'll never get rid of all the glitter. "When you first met me earlier, you gave me a swan."

Silently, he reaches over my shoulder to point to the object that sits on a small nook on the vanity. Huh. I guess I didn't notice it there.

I purse my lips, but then I wonder, "Is that how you see me?"

Rubbing a hand down my hair, he whispers, "Sweet girl."

I give him a small smile. "But not the swan?"

Queran screws his mouth to one side, lips puckering minutely as he debates on how to tell me something without using words. Then, he raises his brows and holds up a finger, signaling for me to wait before he turns around and hastens to a door attached to the bedroom. I wait for a minute or two while he embarks inside. Is that his room? Attached to Bliss's? Well, if he's been her artisan for years, I suppose it's understandable.

Hearing the door click open, I turn to see Queran holding a few different origami shapes—one in his fingers that is a branch; attached to it are tiny, thinner-than-threads branches. On each string of wood are white birds. No bigger than my pinky, but they decorate the branch from the root of its stem to its last point. There must be at least a hundred of them. It had to have taken him days. First, he sets that one aside and then motions to the others inside his cupped hand. A swan. A skeleton flower. A yang. They all brush one another. He tucks the skeleton flower into my ear, places the swan in my hand, and then nestles the yang symbol onto my collarbone. What he does next almost takes my breath away because he takes the branch of birds, touches my chest with one finger, motions to all the birds, and flutters his hand, pretending they are all flying.

I beam up at him. It's the first time I've seen him really smile. It's much fuller than I expected. It accentuates his features like he's turned on twinkle lights underneath his skin so he glows. He might look like a pirate, but he's a sweet pirate. No rogue.

For only one preparation, Queran is altogether perceptive. Or maybe I'm just readable. I guess he did get one thing wrong. Butterflies inside me versus birds. Butterflies always win. They don't peck. And they're far more intelligent. After all, no butterfly tells its offspring to migrate hundreds of miles home before it dies, but somehow, their children still know the way.

Will any of us ever get home?

Will Bliss want to come with us when the time is right?

"Queran." I place the bird branch on the vanity, then stare up at him. "Do you have a shape for my sister?"

Queran holds up his finger again. Patient, I watch him turn to the side and cross the threshold into Bliss's private space. Dangling from a string connected to one of her bedposts is another origami shape, which he untethers before approaching me again. This was shaped years ago. I can tell by the faded gray of the paper, the wear and tear of time. It's a complicated pattern, and I wonder how long it took him to complete it. Full of intersecting triangular folds that all form a complex star—one with gaps so I can see through each one to whatever's on the opposite side. Inside one gap appears a Queran eye, a blue Northern Light ribbon as I hold it up.

Gentle, he takes it from my hand and then begins to shake it, desperate movements, before he shrugs and sticks one finger through the center gap. I read the message loud and clear. Beautiful and intricate on the outside like a convoluted labyrinth, but empty on the inside.

No, I believe there's something more, but if this young man has been preparing my sister for years and seen nothing but this, how can I expect to find something else when we've only just met? Especially when she wants nothing to do with me.

BLISS

TEN YEARS AGO…

"Good girl, Bliss." Force patted my head when we arrived at the Breakable Room.

I'd heard of the Breakable Room. How it was Father's happy place. Once, I'd peeked around the corner when I saw him walk down the hallway to that room. He'd entered, closed the door, and hadn't emerged for an hour. When he had, he hadn't looked like Father. One of his hands had been so red it resembled a giant blister. The ends of his whip had been bloody.

He used to bring Mother there all the time.

But it was the first time he'd brought me there.

After opening the door, Father gave me a little nudge inside. I wanted to leap into the room. It was an honor to be here. Father was sharing a special secret with me. But I wasn't brave enough to leap. Just like I wasn't brave enough to go up to the roof and swim in the pool like he always wanted. I was never brave enough for the pool he built just for me on the first level of our Penthouse. Too caught up with how the water could get all up in my nose and my eyes so I couldn't breathe…I couldn't ride a horse either. Or join Father for skydiving or rock climbing or any of his other daring do's.

Father closed the door behind him.

Confused, I glanced around, wondering what could possibly be so special about this place. There was nothing but glass walls all around us. Even a glass floor, but they were like a magician's mirror. I couldn't see through them at all. All I saw was my own reflection. They were like mirrors.

Father touched my shoulder, then tucked a couple of my curly waves behind my ears, fiddling with the ends around my neck.

"My little girl is growing up," Father pronounced.

I smiled up at him. So often, he spent too much time away from home. Of course, I was always busy. Father made sure I had special tutors for dance and music and acting. I loved acting the most.

"Bliss." Father's hand wandered to the back of my head as he stared down at me. "You perform very well in your acting class from what I've heard."

"Yes, Professor Shurp says I'm a prodigy."

"Good, my love. Tonight, you will perform for me."

"For you?"

"Yes. Think of it as a game. But you must follow the rules, which I set, and you will do everything I tell you to do. Do you understand?"

I bit down on my lip but nodded. "Yes, Father."

"Good girl. You've always been my good girl."

Because all I ever wanted was his happiness.

"Will this make you happy, Father?"

He cupped my chin, lifted it gently, and said, "I hope so, my bit of Bliss. If not…" His eyes strayed to the whip dangling from his belt.

After I performed, it was the last time he ever called me Bliss.

It was the last time I ever saw the inside of the Breakable Room.

It was the first time I felt his whip.

Present

Father has confined Serafina to a suite because he will begin Serenity's training in the Breakable Room. The routine is familiar, so I take the necessary steps to prepare myself. Slipping into the submissive role suddenly seems more difficult. In the past, I've mastered this for my father and for clients because it takes a strong woman to do so, particularly at my age. If the Temple recruiters spoke the truth in ads, they would state the requirements of a Temple girl must include an absent vomiting reflex, penchant for masochism or ability to endure great pain and degradation, suppression of the fight-or-flight instinct, and, most importantly… no tears.

Tonight, for the first time, I recognize I am not completely catering to another person's whims and desires. All other times, I've managed to push mountains in front of my mind and disappear to cope with what my body must endure. Not tonight. I don't want to disappear. I want to feel every whip crack. Donning the skin of a child is risky. It will unearth memories I've long since buried.

Tonight, I become Serafina again. Before, this disappointed him. Now, thanks to Serenity, it won't. I could never become the angel he saw in our mother, but nor could I adopt the dominant demon that burned in his own heart. Little comfort that countless girls couldn't satisfy him either. I came close, but nothing like my mother.

And he punished me for it that night.

That first time, the whip burned. Flaming serpent fangs clawing at my child's flesh—a delicate garment that has since borne the brunt of thousands of different skins. Sometimes, if he has an important client for me, Father will order a session in the regenerator to repair my old scars and bruises or the freshly seared flesh for the times he's punished me. Other times, automatic-skin graft technology if there is no rush because healing still takes longer with grafts—even if the process has quickened from months to days. I wonder if healing will be in store after tonight.

Submission is not unwelcome. So many clients have other needs that are far more complicated. Pain is simple. And real. Serenity won't see what I'm doing. She won't realize this will be an offering. Not a sacrifice. I am giving something of myself.

For once, I'm doing this on behalf of someone else. It's all new, but I don't want to lose it. Father won't see it either, but he never will. Since that night, he gave up seeing anything but a broken girl.

Even if it means my father will destroy my sister in the process, I would rather it was her and not Serafina. I can't lose what I never had to begin with, but now I've met Serafina, now I've spent time with my mother, I can't help but admit my desire to keep her close. I will do whatever it takes to preserve what Father has not destroyed. I will suck the pain so she does not have to.

Fourteen

Training

SERENITY

THE BREAKABLE ROOM.

Though I should've expected nothing less than from my father, it still feels like shards of glass lodged in my throat. They grow larger once Force opens the door and I see my sister kneeling inside, her back to us with nothing but a thin, transparent shift covering her.

"Good girl, Mara," Force commends.

Is my sister's heart like a spider web that our father has spun into his own design? How old was she when he started?

My father turns to face me. "Life is all about balance, Serenity. For every decision we make, there is an opposite that counteracts our own. Dominant—" He motions to us. "Submissive." He points to Bliss. "Giving and receiving. Yin and Yang."

He reminds me of Jade. Her words resound in my head about how submissiveness is never passive. Bliss is the very portrait of submissiveness. Sky was not.

Unlike Jade, Force does not stipulate any boundaries. Nor does he communicate in any way. All he does is withdraw the whip from his jacket and place it in my hand, fully expecting me to use it. A trial by fire. This is more about me than Bliss. There is no respect.

What Jade did was against Sky's will, but it was far different from this.

I hold onto my mother. Nothing else but her face when Force slaughtered my real father. Nothing else but Bliss's voice when she

80

offered herself in our mother's place. *Offered*. Most of all, I try to remember her sacrifice.

When I close my eyes and flick the whip against her back, I understand this isn't about Force. It's about Bliss, Serafina, and me. A triangle.

Force pushes his way inside, voice hardened. "You broke *nothing*."

He's referring to the undamaged shift she wears, the lack of cuts dealt by my hand.

Too impatient, Force rips the whip from my hand, stands next to me, and cracks it against the upper part of Bliss's back, demonstrating. It slices the fabric clean. It snaps her skin in two. She flinches only a little, but I don't see her cringe. No wince in her eyes. Her hands haven't even moved from their folded position in her lap. One garish gash shows Force's success. As well as his mastery of the technique. More so than Jade ever was.

"You have my blood. Start acting like it." After prying open my fingers, he slaps the whip handle into my palm.

Force is the ultimate deceiver because he deceives even himself. I've read my mother's journal. I know the secrets in my father's eyes. For him, the control isn't what he enjoys most. The violence is his drug. The abuse. The *sadism*.

No matter how he dresses it up in dominant words, Force is a sadist through and through. He's punishing Bliss for something. For not being me? Not being like him?

Desperate to find balance, I raise one finger to my father just before approaching Bliss. Then, I kneel beside her.

"Serenity," Force bellows.

"Get *up*." Without moving a muscle, Bliss whispers the words so low Force can't possibly hear.

I ignore my father. I need to tell her. I need her to know.

I whisper in Bliss's ear. "Thank you."

Her exhale is all I need. That she understands where Force has no love for her, no sense of respect or equality, I do. To me, she is the strong one right now. Right now, we are both human. We have equal blood, equal hearts, equal souls. We always have.

I rise to a stand just as Force reaches my side, eyes narrowed to a burn like scorched emeralds. This time, I don't stop. I want to go slow as Jade did, but I know what my father expects. I know Bliss can endure.

"Well done, Serenity." Force admires my stroke when it lands on Bliss's back, creating a line diagonal to the one he'd just formed moments prior. "Each line you create is different. Each mark is a new page to her story. Each one is a badge, a testament to the power you have wrought. Please continue."

Yes, power. That is all it is to him. A power play. All a game.

It's not a game to me. More and more fabric is ripped, but with each new mark, I see other patches of her back where skin has been healed, where previous lines scarred, turned silvery from time. Healed to a certain degree. Skin grafts, I'd wager. How many times has he done this to her? How many clients have taken out their own violent fantasies on her skin?

It feels like Bliss is somewhere between fantasy and reality. She is so beautiful in this moment. Just like Queran's tetra-star shape. Intricately healed scars have mended over each other, paving the way for these new ones from my hand. I'm just adding more paper triangles to her.

Pretending for my father comes simple. Whatever mask I wear, he accepts. So when I pause, step back, and stare at the torn strips of flesh I've inflicted, he takes it as appreciation. He doesn't see it as a delay tactic—a way to draw out the experience with some moments undefined by pain. Does she feel it? My mother wrote about how she wouldn't even feel the pain at times. Or how other times when she became a ghost to the Unicorn, she would welcome the pain because it brought a different form of pleasure with it—knowing she was fulfilling my father's desires.

I want to believe Bliss is not doing this for Force. At the most, she's doing this for our mother. At the very least, she's doing this for herself. Anything but for Force. We can share our mother. I want to know there's something at the end of this rabbit hole. Not just me falling again and again, diving deeper and deeper until there's no hope I can ever crawl out.

I won't become a monster.

Sky would never let that happen.

I must never let that happen.

Fifteen

HeaLing

BLISS

GRIT MY TEETH AFTER THE first strike. Sink my head low, clenching my eyes after the next few. Not every whip crack slices.

Then, my skin begins to soften. Pain grows with every passing second.

I wish she wouldn't stop every few seconds. There's too much space between the strokes. Too many seconds before the next blow lands, taking me by surprise. So many of my clients do not stop. Whether pounding, biting, choking, scratching…beating. What Serenity gives is a rash pain, but it's a quick one. Over all too soon. These few second intervals Serenity deals are driving me mad.

Breathing becomes difficult. The pain fades compared to the necessity to breathe. Every time I feel like I'm ready to pass out, Serenity's whip cuts me again, sending lightning shooting into my organs, causing me to seize up.

"Stop," Force finally cuts her off. "I want to see."

He crosses the floor until he stands behind me. By now, the shift I wear dangles loosely off my skin, held on by a simple ring of fabric around the back of my neck. Instinctively, I wince when Father drags his thumb down one of the open wounds, murmuring in approval. Ten in all.

"Beautiful. Not as deep as mine but a worthy first effort. Look, Serenity. Look at what you've done. Where there is pain, there is also joy. From the pain will come healing, and with healing, there will be strength. You are giving your sister strength."

83

She is giving me nothing. I win that strength on my own. I own it all by myself.

Serenity chooses not to respond. I have no interest in seeing her expression, in reading her emotions. Whether she agrees with him or loathes him for this, I couldn't care less. This isn't about her. It's about me. Her hand caused the damage, but the pain is mine. The aftermath is mine, and she can't share it.

I will not allow it.

"Tomorrow, I will personally take you on a Temple tour," Father announces to Serenity.

I've never left the Penthouse. Serenity will have access to everything. She will take part in exhibits on all levels while I will remain up here—close to the clouds but always in the shadows.

"Get some sleep," he tells her, but I still don't look back at them. "You'll need it."

I hear the door close, but I can still sense her behind me. Sighing finally, I perform utterly slow movements as I try to get to my feet.

"Bliss—"

She starts to touch my arm, but I flick just my head at her and snap, "I don't want your help."

"Bliss, I-I was trying to make it—"

"There is nothing easy about it." I manage to keep any emotion under the surface. "There is no way to soften the blow. You don't understand. You'll never understand."

I pause to take stock of her expression. In her eyes, I read guilt, sympathy. Damn, I read pity. Then, it all shifts. Her features screw tighter, eyes and lips contorting. Good, anger I can handle. It's an inferior emotion. It just proves I'm stronger than her.

"I'm *not* him."

I deadpan. "No, you're much worse."

WHEN I STEP INTO MY suite, I expect to find Queran. Father normally assigns him to heal me after client appointments. While I do find him, Serafina is also standing there. All the healing remedies along with the skin grafter sit on a small table near the mirror. I don't know how long she's been waiting, but once I see the origami objects in Queran's hand, I know she must have been waiting for me during all of Serenity's training.

He holds up the tiny unicorn shape, then gestures to her and to the healing remedies.

I nod with a soft sigh. "Just for tonight, Queran."

Reluctant, Queran nods, squeezing my hand once before departing.

"Just for tonight," I repeat to my mother, reminding her.

"Lie down on the bed, Bliss."

My mother offers no other words, just the simple directions. She understands exactly what I need. I imagine she had her own healer. Perhaps she went through more than just one. Father isn't the type to heal. He would have hired multiple healers for Serafina.

At least Queran's hands are equally masterful at healing.

He was shy at first. Though I was still young at the time, healing was a more intimate service than preparing. By now, it's second nature for us. Serafina's hands are patient but still different from Queran's soft, steadfast ones. For my mother, the tables have turned. I sense the way her fingers experiment with my skin, lingering even after she's applied a salve to numb and antiseptic.

Finally, she trains the skin grafter on my open flesh. A moment later, I smell the lasers patching my skin.

I'm grateful she asks no questions. Then again, why would she? She's lived through this. But never at the hands of her own flesh and blood. That is where we differ. I suppose Force was altogether a different sort of bond. Perhaps even closer. I know that bond still exists on some level. Even if the strings binding them together are raw and tattered, they still exist. No one can ever escape Father. So much more than a ghost, he becomes one's own personal poltergeist.

"She did well," I say after a few minutes.

"Don't," my mother requests as she finishes the process, eyes focused on my back.

"It was my choice."

It's the first time I've made my mother pause. It's the first time I've seen her gaze more than just contemplative, patient, loving, or even understanding when she stares at me. In fact, it's resentful.

"It wasn't yours to make," she says, voice deliberate.

"You didn't *want* to. I did."

"It's not your responsibility."

"It's not about responsibility." I set my chin on the pillow. "Father has been a part of me for a long time. Longer than the stretch of time he spent with you. I understand him on a level you never will. I will never fall into the snare of needing him like you would. I keep him at bay. I keep them all at bay."

Serafina sighs as if doubting my words.

"And what about Serenity?" At least she doesn't argue with my last statement.

I don't look at her. "What about her?"

"She is your sister."

I shake my head.

"Will you always keep her at bay?"

When I don't respond, Serafina sighs, and I wonder if she understands why I refuse to really see the girl who wears my face.

"Serenity has her faults. She has her father's blood, but she is *not* him."

Out of the corner of my eye, I glance at her. At the words she's repeated that earlier came from Serenity's mouth.

Serafina purses her lips and stares up at the ceiling, weighing words, narrowing down which ones she wants to use. "Serenity may be a butterfly flying in a storm. But she always comes back to the earth. She has *something* that grounds her. She won't let Force lead her astray. She won't fly straight into the lightning."

I remember the girl's face inside the Breakable Room. I remember the anger striking a chord on her features when I'd refused her help because she thought it was something she could fix. Oh, her arrogance in thinking we could ever share anything but DNA! Perhaps if I saw more of Serafina in her, but there is not enough to reckon with. Father and his pride are strongest in her. Now that we are all in the Temple, our mother will see soon enough.

Serenity can never be both parents like me.

She will always see the world through fire-colored glasses.

Sixteen

My NeSt

SERENITY

KY FEELS LIKE THE NEST I come home to. He is waiting for me in the middle of my room. Luc is with him. Glad to see they're tolerating each other.

When I enter the bedroom, I imagine I must look as haggard as I feel. Without bothering to shake the curls loose from both sides of my face, I take slow, single-minded steps in a straight line until I've reached my destination. His arms come around me, reminding me of their sanctuary even while I want to resist the healing.

I flick my gaze over at Luc, and Sky juts one finger at the door. "Out."

Luc does not argue with his brother, for which I'm thankful. I'd like to believe it's because he recognizes how much I need Sky right now, but I doubt it.

"Talk to me, Ser."

Yes, talk. Words are necessary. Kerrick's death was different. Now, I need to sort out my thoughts, reckon with my emotions, face the consequences.

"She hates me. I don't blame her."

"I don't either. I blame that parasite of your father."

I make my way to the bed and slump onto it, shoulders heavy. "It's more than that. It might have started with him, but she's built up a wall around herself. Having to play my father in the Breakable Room just makes it *thicker*. How am I supposed to get through to her when I'm supposed to 'become like him'?"

Shrugging, Sky collapses onto the bed beside me, legs hanging halfway off to the floor. "Guess you try three times as hard when he's not around."

I lie next to him, ease my head onto his shoulder, and peer up at the sprite light canopy. The one with a tranquil lake scene with ambiance noises of crickets and bullfrogs. I smile. Sky must have chosen it. I raise a finger toward the water, discovering how the canopy lowers at my body's motion. My father's feature, I'd wager. The corner of the scene offers an option to change the programming. I summon up the canopy's internet capabilities, sweeping my finger to a host of apps.

Sky snorts next to me.

"What?" I glance at him.

He jerks his head, points to an app. "Pleasyour." He says the app name, which sounds like a butchering of "pleasure". "I've heard of it. Must be Force's little present. It'll send energy pulses in the form of pleasure wavelengths into your body." He selects the app, shows how I can choose any setting and any model or story I want. Countless celebrities and models make up the repertoire. Sky and I start going through the gallery, laughing at the cheesy stories.

"Come on, Sky," I tease, elbowing his side. "You know you'd totally want the naughty maid who knew too much." I gesture to the exotic mystery story.

Sky chuckles, bantering with me. "How about him?" He pulls up the profile of a muscular knight from medieval times, who kneels and holds a rose. "He seems interesting. Description: Heroic, romantic, worships at your feet, will perform any command you desire. The sky is the limit. Hmm…" He trails off before nudging our foreheads together. "Seriously, are you curious, Ser?"

I flick my hand up to turn off the canopy. "No. I want my first time to be with you."

It came out so fast I shouldn't wonder why Sky appears a little surprised himself. I can't think about it all right now. Not with how close his body is. Or how in this light, the dark muslin in his eyes wraps me in warmth.

So, I whisper, "Have you figured anything out yet?"

Sky sighs, staring up at the canopy. "I could get you and your sister out but not your mother. She'd want you to go."

"I won't. Not without her. And Bliss won't either."

"The implant link is recent technology. I'm still researching what I can find. It can't be hacked remotely because it's connected to Force's personal interface. It has to be tampered with manually. And there's no telling where the implant is located inside him."

"So, it's pretty much impossible." I throw my hands in the air before dragging my nails into my scalp. "What if I'm not strong enough for this? What if I start to become him?"

He blows out a breath through his nostrils, upsetting a couple of wavy tendrils of his hair in the process. "Would like to say it won't happen because you have me. But it'd be a lie." Sky turns so our noses bump, so his eyes peer dead into mine. "I'll be here for you like always. But you gotta fight it, too. I can't do it for you. We all got our own demons we gotta wrestle. Came to grips with my own in that Shed just like you did yours. Guess you'll be facing your biggest demon here."

I cup my forehead. "That's an understatement."

"Hey," he says, and I turn with a sigh. "Stay with me, Ser. I'll always come for you. Just ask that you stick around."

"I'm not going anywhere."

Sky shifts our bodies. Folds us under the covers, saddling me against his body, nestling his arms around my waist and creating a cocoon of our combined body heat.

When I wake in the morning, he's returned to the rafters. It's cold without him, but I still smell him on my skin, so I hang onto that even when my father's voice calling me for breakfast sours my appetite.

Seventeen

TemPle ToUr

SERENITY

"THIS IS THE MERMAID EXHIBITION Level."

Force reveals this singular level to me in his extravagant sky-city. It's a higher level, and he's saved it as one of the last exhibit levels he will show me today. A closer, more in-depth tour will occur later tonight. I don't bother telling him I'd rather stay in the Penthouse. After all, any information I can give to Sky will be helpful. Mentally, I try to catalogue all the security details I can: the temporary barcode every visitor is required to have upon entry, the sensor-driven glass gates that scan each barcode to determine if patrons have paid for a certain level or interaction—credits, of course—the Black Hand security guards scattered throughout each level. Naturally, more monitor the higher ones along with drones. Two accompany Director Force on every level but the Penthouse. Their shadows have hovered behind us all this time.

Up ahead, I get a glimpse of the first exhibit and feel over-dressed again. Just like I did in Arabia Land. Or Ballerina Land. Or Beach Land. The last took up entire lower levels and boasted a real sand beach and a wave pool with a solar-driven backdrop to simulate an ocean horizon. My father boasted about the palm trees he'd imported from tropical locations.

Upon entering the mermaid level, we pass a receptionist's desk strategically placed before any of the displays. On either side of the desk are frosted glass gates that prevent viewers from entering until they've scanned their barcodes. She doesn't look up on our initial approach as she studies the holographic screen in front of her, narrow-framed spectacles perched on her equally narrow-bridged nose.

"Welcome to Mermaid Land. Would you like to schedule a personal tour or interaction?" she drones, monotonous.

"Good morning, Rhonda."

Immediately, she straightens and leaps out of her chair, upsetting a coffee mug before scrambling around to the other side. "Director Force! My deepest apologies. I wasn't expect—"

"Come now, Rhonda, I don't bite," he tells her while scooping up her hand to kiss it.

Rhonda is much older than me. I'd wager closer to my father's age, and I wonder why he's arranged for someone more advanced in years as a receptionist and tour guide. She manages a half smile, and I sense a history between them. Considering how many girls my father has taken to his bed, it doesn't surprise me that he would have sampled a wide variety.

"Do you need a personal tour?" she offers, but Force raises a hand.

"No, thank you. We won't be long since lunchtime is approaching. Please don't forget clients still grace our halls during the day hours, slower though it may be."

"Yes, Director Force. We have many interactions scheduled for this evening, and—"

"I understand, but this place must run like a well-oiled machine. Do not forget what happens to parts that cannot perform." His voice lowers an octave on that last note, tone like a bristling porcupine, reminding one of its needles.

She lowers her head, and he dismisses her. For her, I can tell the receptionist's desk is more like a bubble. Considering he didn't bother to make an introduction, I know he counts her as no more than a bug he may squash at any time.

My father taps his temple, both sides of his mouth curling as the frosted gates open before him. Proud as a jester with peacock feathers to preen. "I used to have interface lenses, but they would be far too simple for my enemies to steal and manipulate. A neural interface is far more effective."

"Anything you're pondering?" He escorts me down the hall. Designed as such for lines, but tanks line each side filled with exotic species of fish.

Oh, you know, trying to keep a log of everything I've learned so I can later use it to escape or so I can use it against you.

"All your receptionists are older. Why?"

"A simple question with a simple answer: I prefer my exhibit lovelies to be the main spectacle. I do not detract from them in any way."

"But in the main lobby—"

"The processing center is different," he interrupts, staring back at me every so often but not at any tank. "One must keep up appearances. Having worthy girls checking clients in keeps them more intrigued. If those girls are simply ones who act as directional guides, then what are the exhibit ones like?"

I suppose there weren't too many girls in the lobby. Everything was automated from barcode machines to screens allowing someone to customize their visits for the day—what levels they would pay for, how much time they would stay, and if they wanted to pay extra for an interaction. Digital advertisements only served to tease clients more, providing them with tidbits of information regarding the higher levels—a method used to seduce credits straight from their barcodes. Yearly sponsors are provided complimentary access to one level for the duration of the year. Lifetime sponsors get full access including behind the scenes interactions and extended services of their choosing.

Up till now, I haven't asked many questions. Exhibits have proven too distracting, much like this one now as we come to the entryway.

The first two displays are simple rectangular boxes resting behind glass-barred gates, preventing any sense of full access to the girls. These girls have simple prosthetic tails and similar additions to the rest of their body. They alternate between climbing into the water-filled boxes to swim only to issue out and sit on top as if they are sunning themselves. With the solar lights imitating the sun above our heads and the ambience of ocean waves, it's not difficult to picture.

However, my father doesn't linger here. Here, there is a system. Exhibits become more complex the more we progress. Displays continue to grow, adding touches of coral, seaweed, oceanic rock formations. The final exhibit is an ostentatious tank with a backdrop of a glittering sunken palace. More than one mermaid frequents this.

Once I cross over to examine the mermaids inside—the attention to detail paid to their prosthetics and makeup from the symmetrical scales on their legs to the prosthetics joining their feet. Some have coral prosthetics or octopi-like suckers so they truly become part of an oceanic world. Blue hair for a few, green for another—no color left untouched. A couple have shells to decorate their privates. Scales, pearls, or jewels house others while a couple don't have anything but their serpentine hair mushrooming into the water. They all swim down to my level, pointing and gesturing, hands spread against the glass. I turn to see my father watching with an amused smirk, hands folded behind him.

"Your underwater dance the other night has become an overnight sensation. My mermaids are eager for you to join them." When he sweeps a finger against the glass, one girl flirts with him, spinning around in a teasing manner.

None of them surface. A never-ending supply of bubbles continue to trickle up from their noses.

Puzzled, I narrow my brows, waiting for an explanation.

"My beauties here are equipped with built-in oxygen devices."

Spreading my hand to theirs, I dream of the possibility. To actually breathe underwater!

"Naturally, I cannot allow you to swim in dual exhibits. You will always have your own private one. Ahh, that would be Jewel."

Startled at the sudden creature sashaying through the water, back end bobbing up and down, I hurry to catch up to her shape as she swims past the other mermaids. Their fingers tickle across her sleek back, the steel gray of her skin and fins. Her eternal smile lodges in my memory, the familiar whistles and chirps I remember waking to one childhood morning we spent in my parents' seaside villa.

My father cups my shoulders as I stare at the dolphin. "Would you like to swim with Jewel, Serenity? My beauties here are trained to do so for exhibits, but I can certainly arrange for you to have an experience."

To breathe underwater while swimming with a dolphin.

THE TEMPLE

The Temple's lasso tightens.

"WE HAVE ONE LEVEL DEDICATED to the different seasons. I'm certain you would enjoy Winter," he says knowingly.

More of a summer person, but I can take winter as long as there's a way to swim inside like a hotel indoor pool. Summers with my family at our lakeside manor were the best times. Summer days swimming in the water, nights curled up by the fire. Winters in hotels were the best. Wool sweaters snuggled my neck and hid my curves as I watched the snow fall outside the windows while Sky and I sneaked into the pools after midnight to swim.

The elevator doors open.

"This one is another personal favorite of mine," Force tells me.

This time, Force has chosen an employees' entrance into the main wing on the opposite side of the receptionist desk. As soon as I step inside, I notice movement on my right from behind glass. Inside is a young girl no more than fourteen with an ensemble of eye makeup that runs in strategic drips from her eyes that emphasizes weeping. Flecking the end of each tear-line is a tiny diamond. She wears nothing but a transparent white dress. While the rest of her exhibit is pitch black, a spotlight dazzles her form wherever she walks, casting a dim glow around her outline. As soon as she moves, her wings appear. Great, feathered, and black as nightshade and nightmares.

"This is Angel Land," Force declares, sweeping a hand to the floor.

Some girls wander in exhibits clothed in nothing more than white feathery wings and lacy lingerie. One exhibit is a featured one, the signature for the month—labeled Fallen Angel. Pupils dilated so much it looks like they've swallowed her irises. Black veins web out from random areas of her eyes and the corners of her blue-tinted mouth, resembling thin sinister branches. Nothing but a black rose for each of her breasts. On the ground all around her are clumps of feathers splattered by blood. Off to the right exhibit side, I see a wing lying there, plucked and discarded like an unwanted doll. When she turns around, the black tea skin of her bare back reveals one long jagged gash where the wing has been severed. The injury drips blood I'm certain is a result of some timed-device that is meant to drip every few minutes or so.

"That is my Naamah," Force designates, gesturing to the exhibit. "I use her as a standing exhibit for this month every year, unveiling her for public display now and only now. If clients request her any other time of the year, it must be only as a private interaction. Trust me, many do."

Naamah's fingers are crusted in blood. As part of her display, she reaches one arm behind her until her fingers land on what she has lost. The one sacred wing she has left coddles the left side of her body like a scabbard longing to cover its sword. She is a weapon. A weapon with tortuous curves and lost eyes any man would want to hunt down for two lifetimes.

"Isn't Naamah the fallen angel of prostitution?" I sarcastically quip as the girl behind the glass kneels to gather up her forsaken feathers.

"Well now, someone has studied her mythology."

"I went through an angel phase," I excuse. It was a pet name my father always gave to my mother.

"Hmm…these beauties are not so rare anymore. After all, even the early days of our culture associated angels with modeling lingerie and undergarments."

"A poor representation to the reality of angels."

"Reality? What a surprise my own daughter should blur the lines between magic and realism."

Tightening my fists, I confront my father. "Some are made of nothing but fire. Others are nothing but shadows and death. No one could ever see or hear them coming. One angel can strike down hundreds."

"Fascinating, really. Ahh, Neil."

My father motions to a figure behind me. I turn around to see my half-brother sauntering toward us, Luc following behind him. Keeping something behind his back, Neil stops just before me, eyes landing on Naamah's exhibit for a moment.

"I trust everything is in order, son?" Force addresses Neil.

"Just as you ordered."

Neil produces a small screen that features a national magazine cover image of me underwater from my Swan/Skeleton Flower grand opening. When he swipes the screen, multiple covers reveal others. One of me in the boat, one of me with a hand fanned out on the glass, one of me surfacing—Neil outdid himself. Despite his finger swiping, his eyes aren't focused on me but on Naamah.

"Excellent," Force commends him before glancing at Luc. "And how are the next stages coming along?"

Unlike Neil's casual manner, Luc keeps his hands at his side. So rigid, they've practically transformed into stakes. "The next exhibit's final draft is finished," he replies in a stony voice.

I spin back to my father. "What is the next exhibit?"

Grinning, he reaches out to tap my nose. "Now, do you honestly believe I would tell you that, my dear?"

"When?"

"Next week. I prefer to draw out your exhibits. But that does not mean you have free time every evening. In fact, I think I'll have Luc join us for lunch since you will be otherwise engaged for dinner."

I grit my teeth. "I don't want him to come for lunch."

Force eyes Luc from the side before flicking his gaze to me. "Don't be foolish. This show of play is pointless, though I am curious to ascertain what is driving its source. Rest assured, I will learn.

"Now, Neil, if you can manage to clean up the river of drool left in your wake from staring at Naamah, I trust you and Luc can escort Serenity back to her room for lunch. I will be there shortly." When Neil doesn't respond, our father huffs, "Honestly, boy, just bed her already. I'll even give you an interaction on the house."

Force doesn't give me the chance to argue more. I groan, frustrated. Even more frustrated because Luc didn't bother to object to the lunch date.

Neil is still staring at Naamah.

Taking advantage of the distraction, I poke him in the side. "Ow!"

"Baby." I stick out my tongue before turning to stand next to him. After screening his eyes that have for once lost all their charm, I surmise, "She's the one, isn't she? Let me guess, you've never photographed her."

He shakes his head. "My lens could never do her justice." His eyes follow her, dance along every curve as she moves, even as she descends into a tragic kneel, neck arched, eyes crying to the heavens.

"You could always schedule an interaction and just talk to her," I suggest. "Like you did with me."

"Serenity." Neil rolls his eyes, then gazes at Naamah again as she wanders toward the back of the exhibit, bare feet smoothing across the polished floor. "No one talks in the Temple. It's for secrets and fantasies. Nothing more. What happens in the Temple…"

Denial sounds weak coming from Neil's mouth. Perhaps there really is more to him than meets the eye.

"She is statuesque in a way," Luc notes. "Nothing like Serenity's ferocious allure."

"Stop," I warn him.

"You two go on ahead. I'll…be…right there." Neil waves us off, and it's clear he intends to take his time. I bet he'll miss the appetizer course.

"Let's go," Luc says.

He tries to take my elbow, but I refuse him and step forward on my own. It doesn't take him long to fall into stride with me.

He sighs as we approach the elevator. "I'm used to pursuing challenges, not forsaking them."

"I'm not a challenge, Luc. No girl should be. We're not conquests."

We reach the elevator. Luc has a barcode that provides him access to all levels including the Penthouse. Once the doors close, he finally speaks.

"Yes, you are," Luc contradicts.

"Excuse me?" I exclaim, doing a double take.

Luc stops the elevator. Advances toward me. Instead of backing up against the corner, I retaliate. Familiar with my habits, he knows better because he manages to wrestle my aggressive hand and pin it behind my back just before his other follows suit. I continue to struggle.

"Every man has a deep, stirring need to conquer. It is one reason why wars are fought." Luc murmurs in my ear, voice bordering on smoky. I can almost sense fumes coming from my ears when he continues, "Despite how simple it is for men to order any girl, their deepest desire is to win one. It's why so many are never satisfied. It's why Neil refuses to bed Naamah. Paying for her is far too easy. Love is always a battlefield."

"You lost the war, Luc," I seethe.

"There are no rules in war," he informs me. "Or love for that matter. All is fair. Even theft."

"You're a fool."

"Perhaps." Leaning in, Luc sweeps aside my hair from my shoulder to reveal his silver brand. "But I noticed you stopped struggling against me."

I pause, realizing the truth of his statement. Oh, well. Hindsight's twenty-twenty. Kicking my legs up against the wall, I use the pressure to throw my whole body back and drive him against the opposite wall. His grip on me loosens as well as his balance, and we tumble to the floor, but I use the moment to punch the button. Clearly unfinished with the discussion due to his obsessive need to have the last word, Luc tries again, but I position myself right in front of the panel, guarding it, lightning ready to pounce.

Luc drags a hand through his hair, eyes pinching. "Back away."

"Not on your life."

"Fitting." He steps toward me. "You'll be the death of me."

"Gladly," I shout just as the elevator doors open to the second level of the Penthouse.

As soon as Luc tries to close the distance between us, I duck and slide into the hall, catching up the ends of my skirt so I can run, grateful I'm in bare feet. Shoes have never been much of a necessity for me. I reach my bedroom just before Luc catches up to me.

My hand touches the knob, but I only get one second to turn it.

"We aren't done yet," Luc commands, ripping my arm away and shoving me against the wall.

I gasp when he pins me there, reminded of the one heated night where he almost took his fill of me. "Fine. We'll talk inside. Oh, that's right, you're too much of a coward," I hurl the word at him.

"Fool, coward—sticks and stones, Serenity. You're denying what's right in front of you."

"That's right! And I'll keep denying it and chase everything else that really matters. And if you weren't so *thick*, if you had one ounce of decency, you'd respect—" His mouth comes down on mine, lips trying to peel mine back. "Luuuu!" I weasel my face to the side, but my cry comes out only halfway before his mouth wrestles with mine again.

I close my eyes and endure, chomping down on all the sensations stirring inside me. The feelings swirl in my stomach, giving my butterflies dizzying dreams, but they try to right themselves through it all. They cling desperately to the inner linings of my stomach walls, wanting so much to stay grounded even as Luc plunders my mouth senseless, tasting me for the first time in weeks.

Once he pauses, creating a gap of no more than a millimeter between us, I try to move, but he keeps my hands settled so far against the wall they become fossilized there. The rest of his body is my pitfall. It seals me into its snare. But no matter how much he tries to inject his ice into me, it doesn't penetrate unlike before. My butterflies easily shake the frost dust from their wings.

I roll my eyes. "Are you done?"

Annoyed, Luc tries once more, and I groan into his mouth. His determination is the weakness I need because when he lowers his hands to cup my face, I take the opportunity. History repeats itself. I've come to appreciate the way my nails can shed his blood.

"You don't think I won't tell Sky?" I threaten when he shrinks away from my attack.

He applies pressure to the scratches. In the next moment, his eyes blister. "No, you won't."

"Oh?"

"You won't take the risk. Because you know what he'll do. And you don't want your father to know." Luc wipes away some of my blood right before approaching me again. "Trust me, Serenity, I've considered telling him, but I won't. Again, challenges are what we desire most. And I have patience in spades. I'll enjoy working to convince you."

"If you want to keep whatever little respect I have for you, you'll stop this now." I raise a stern finger. "It's only going to take you down a deep, dark hole you'll never come back from."

Luc's shadow towers over me as he utters, "As long as I take you with me, I don't care."

Both our heads turn at the sound of a one-man audience clapping for us. "Bravo! Excellent form, Aldaine."

I taste bile in my throat from Force's presence. Wait! Alarm sends my butterflies scrambling. Luc and I both mentioned Sky. How much had Force heard?

"I wish I'd caught the beginning of the interlude, but even the last few moments were a delightful treat," my father comments as he glides toward us. "Perhaps we will discuss some avenues over lunch."

Force opens the door for me.

Eager to be as far from Luc as possible, I hurry inside but pause, capturing the edge of the door with my hand. Then, I face the two of them and announce, "I've got an avenue. It ends with both of you out of my *life*!"

After I slam the door in their faces, I press my ear to the door to hear my father chuckle, "Chip off the old block, that's for certain. Oh well, come now, my boy. We will enjoy a lunch together. Rest assured, I have a solution to this whole business."

My solution is standing at the top of the stairs.

Unfortunately, Luc was right about one thing. I won't take the risk of telling Sky anything about his brother's actions. If there was a guarantee he wouldn't do anything hotheaded, maybe, but it's a possibility, especially with him stuck in the rafters every day.

Before I take another step, I overhear Force.

"What? I'll be right there."

A pause.

"Lunch will need to be postponed."

His voice edges away, and I crack the door just enough so I can hear the rest of the conversation.

"If you'll come with me, Luc, there is a situation where I could use your expertise."

Luc doesn't accompany my father just yet. Stopping a few steps away, Force turns to face the former director.

"And what expertise is that?"

"Why, the art of killing. Naturally."

"And why would you require my expertise in that particular field?"

"More like your reflections. A girl has been murdered on level twelve."

No.

Invisible hands choke all my butterflies. I close the door, sink to the floor, then burrow my face in my knees.

Not again.

PART
Two

Eighteen

DeJaVu

LUC

"SHE WAS BOUND," I REMARK as I bend to examine the body, which lies face down on the glass floor. "You can see the chafing on her wrists." I circle the area above them without touching her.

Using a pen, I sweep aside her hair to study her neck, confirming my suspicions based on her skin palette. "There are signs of strangulation, indicating a necessity for control over the victim."

"Good observations thus far, Aldaine."

It astounds me how that man can pay compliments at a time like this. Always playing the charming director mask despite my knowing the contrary. I suppose we all don them in some form or other. I have my own, but at least I'll admit it.

"I need gloves." I turn to look over at Force, who squats next to me. "Don't you have a forensic pathologist or medical examiner on staff?"

"Retainer," he clarifies. "Situations like this don't occur too often. Naturally, accidents happen in the line of duty for girls here, and we avoid the negative publicity and compensate the families if such families exist. In this case, Star Fruit—" he gestures to the victim, "—was one of my Exhibit Girls of the Year. There is one for each level."

It doesn't surprise me. We had our own system at the Aviary with girls who had performed more admirably than others and rose to become Higher Birds. None such as Serenity. Just beckoning the Aviary memories where she was under my control and not her sadistic father's stirs the killer inside of me. My greatest regret is the auction since it didn't make a damn bit of difference anyway. She walked right through the doors of the Temple.

"What do you think, Aldaine?" Force diverts my attention. Necessary at present. "Jealous rival? Obsessive client? Lustful guard?"

"What about the security cameras?"

"None for this particular area." He circles a finger around the back employee stairwell. "Higher levels are equipped with better security."

It does not necessarily mean the killer was employed with the Temple. With proper motivation, an obsessive client could easily determine what avenues don't have as much security.

"What about other areas? What was her schedule like today?"

"She was off-duty until later this evening. Exhibits of the Year are only featured once a month, and it shifts for each level. Star Fruit could have been in her dressing room or on any other level for all we know. Why?"

"She was not killed here."

"And how do you know that?"

"The angle of the body, how she was placed—they are all wrong. Her hair is also damp as well as her clothes, which could be a result from drowning, but there is no water in the stairwell other than directly around the body." I trace the outlines of the corpse. "A lung 'float test' during the autopsy will help determine whether she was killed by strangulation or by drowning."

"We have well over a hundred pools in this complex."

"Don't forget whirlpools or private baths or on rare occasions even sinks or toilets."

"My thanks. I hadn't thought of that. I will have my security team begin scanning the footage."

I consider offering my own man as a security consultant, but it's not the time for a risk, even a calculated one. By now, I know to make such decisions with my brother.

"What we do know is she wasn't attending to a private interaction," Force offers. "Her last one ended hours ago, and I interrogated him myself. Close ties to the Syndicate."

"Name?"

"Tristan Teane."

I stiffen at the recollection of the man who kissed Serenity upon her first interaction. Though I was not present, I still heard about the encounter from one of the other business associates, who I knew from my Aviary days.

"With your permission, I'd prefer to interrogate Tristan myself."

Force taps his jaw. "I suppose that could be arranged. What about the body itself? The choice of dress? White is not Star Fruit's color."

"Ritualistic or symbolic perhaps," I opt when I consider the soaked material that is eerily similar to the fashion stipulated for Serenity in the Aviary.

"Sexually assaulted?"

"I'd prefer gloves to turn the body over to check."

Force snaps his fingers to one of the guards, who removes his black ones. "They will do while we wait for the medical examiner." He hands them to me.

Donning these gloves feels like second nature despite my father severing me from the Guild. Every time I slide them on, I sit on the artist inside me, push him far down while another part of me may operate whether director or assassin. My gloves become my mask.

Taking the girl by the arms, I shift her body until she's lying on her back, keeping my eyes on her thighs. Edging the damp fabric up, I examine the skin there.

"I don't see any bruises or signs of vaginal laceration, but a bodily fluids analysis will have to be completed. Nor do I see any other bruising signs elsewhere on her body, on her arms or—"

I pause when I observe red marks on her chest, muted beneath the fabric of her dress.

"What is it?"

Leaning over, I tug down on the fabric of her dress to see the scored image resting between her cleavage. A series of colorful curses erupts in my mind, but I only mutter one of them.

"Our lives just became much more complicated." I gesture him over with one finger.

"Damn it to hell!" Force is not so concerned over propriety. Not that I can blame him.

Carved into this girl's chest is a small but definable swan.

Nineteen

SeraFina's SecOnd SkIn

SERENITY

AFTER A WEEK SPENT IN limbo, I'm ready to tear out my hair. Sure, I have access to the rooftop pool and all the entertainment I desire including the private shows my father has arranged for us to enjoy each night during dinner. Of course, he's also arranged suitors for every night, but I've turned each one down, coming up with a colorful way to do so every time. Unfortunately, neither he nor Luc have revealed any details about the murder despite my pressure. No, Luc has been avoiding me since our last encounter. Much like Bliss.

"Give her time," my mother tells me as we eat our lunch together in my suite.

"You keep saying that, but I don't think it will make any difference. How do you know Force hasn't ruined her for good?"

"Bliss isn't ruined," Mom denies. "She's *retreated*. She just needs to be reached. You can't push or lure her out. She must come out in her own time and of her own accord."

"But Kerrick—"

"Never forced me," she interrupts. "He pursued, but he never pushed. He always waited."

Sighing, I look down at my soup. "I'm not very good at waiting."

"Yes, I'm keenly aware of that."

I decide to redirect the topic. "It's been a week. How are you doing without him?"

My mother takes a bite of her salad before staring out the

window. She finally says, "I'd rather not talk about it."

"Why?"

"Leave it alone, Serenity."

"Do you talk to her about it?"

My mother levels with me. "Don't turn it into a competition. You are both my daughters."

"We both *need* you," I emphasize.

"In different ways," my mother adds.

"Does she need you more?" I know I'm trying too hard, but there is something about Bliss my mother understands. Something about my mother Bliss understands. Shared commonalities I'm working too hard to comprehend.

Mom shakes her head. "She needs me less. And that is why I'm spending more time with her. Plus, I know how to delegate."

We both smile, glancing up to my room where Sky has been hiding. During the day, he'll disappear for hours here and there, but he always returns.

"Are you almost finished down there?" he calls in a faint voice. "I'm hungry."

Rolling my eyes, I pick up the extra soup bowl I ordered. "You're always hungry," I announce just before heading for the stairs.

"Why don't you ever come down?" I ask once I step inside the room. "There are no cameras in the entire suite."

"I won't risk it," he replies, standing in the center of the room to welcome me. "Not with your father's complete disregard for knocking. Thank you." He nods when I present him with the soup.

Just then, I hear the door click open from downstairs. I signal Sky to return to the rafters while I grab a binder for my hair—the only excuse I can come up with for why I'd be upstairs but my mother downstairs.

"Good afternoon, Serenity," Force says when I start heading down the staircase.

He doesn't even acknowledge my mother. Good.

"Nice to see you occupying your time without complaint."

He's dressed casually today. If casual can ever define my father. With his sleeves rolled up, I can see his tattoos up close for the first time. The unicorn doesn't surprise me. I assume the swan must be a more recent one. Both digital. The unicorn's horn glows. She shakes her mane while the swan curves her neck and flutters her wings a few times. The Yin/Yang symbol must lie elsewhere. The stubble above his upper lip and around his chin has grown more. One point of fashion he rarely ever loses are the scarf scraps he keeps tied around his neck or the randomized rips in his clothing. He enjoys ripping apart people. Why shouldn't his own clothes follow suit?

"You will report to Level 189's Preparation Room promptly at five PM. Understood?"

"Will Lindy be there?"

Clearly pleased at my inquiry, Force folds his hands behind his back and smiles. "I can arrange it. She appeals to your palette?"

Shrugging, I take a sip of water as he reaches the side of the table. "Not as much as Queran, but—"

"Queran? Now that is a surprise. After your initial reaction, I thought I would have to drag you to your next interaction kicking and screaming."

"He grows on you." For the past week, I stayed for Bliss's preparations. Every time, Queran created a new shape for me. I've begun to collect them. A worthy substitute to my absent snow globes.

"That he does."

My father glances at my mother, and I almost hiss at the invasion.

"Force."

I do hiss then but at my mother this time. "Mom!"

"No," she snaps at me, scooting out of her chair. "I won't have him ignoring me. I'm a human being, and I have my own rights to be seen and heard."

"You don't have to—" I stand to say, but she cuts off the air between us and slices my words in two.

"Step aside, Serenity." We are on eye level with one another, but for the first time, my mother's gray eyes become the warships I've observed but have never felt up until now. She's never used them on me. Not once. "You can play your father with Bliss but not with me."

Her words gut me. Like sharp canine incisors chopping my

110

butterfly wings until they decorate the bottom of my stomach worse than wood shavings in a hamster cage. Shifting my weight, I bite down on my lower lip and then step to the side, obeying my mother.

"Force."

I watch her turn to face him. It makes me cringe just to see him take a step toward her.

"How does it feel?" he wants to know. "My name on your tongue as opposed to director?"

"It doesn't matter how anything feels. It only matters you listen and understand."

He raises a fist to his chin before waving to her. "Go on."

"You might plan everything down to the last detail like you always do, but I can make plans, too. Make no mistake, Force. If you hurt either of my daughters any more in any way, I will kill you. Even if it means I kill myself in the process, I won't let you destroy *my* children."

I let out the breath I'm holding. Her words have breathed life back into my butterflies, and they are clapping their wings, giving her a round of applause. Antennae are vibrating. They're singing her praises straight into my heart.

"Hmm." My father regards her for a moment. "It seems I did trade one addiction for another. Old habits die hard, but I'll never be able to fulfill them again with you, will I? You've shed yourself, Serafina." He raises a knowing finger. "Adopted a second skin, I'd say. Suppose the fault does lie with me."

"You merely set the stage. I chose my own course," my mother maintains. "I chose it the day I left the Temple. I chose it every day since. Whatever happens from now on, you can't hurt me."

"I believe you." Another chaotic grin creases the corners of his mouth. "But I certainly would enjoy trying."

My mother's eyes fire their warship cannons. "And I would let you, provided you give up on your latest addiction."

I hold my breath again. My butterflies have formed a division. A civil war erupting in my stomach. One side rationalizing for my mother's decision because she is the parent and protector, and I'm the child. This is her right.

The other side is resilient. *Think of what he will do to her,* they tell me. *She doesn't deserve that. Not after all she's done for you. Not after all she and Kerrick have done for other girls through the years.*

Bliss doesn't deserve it either.

No girl does.

She bears it better than others, doesn't she? She can bear it more than my mother, right?

"No." My father resolves the war for me. "Thank you for the offer, but I prefer my new addiction more. Besides, it affords me a legacy that will be fulfilled. Grooming a new director takes time after all." His eyes flick to mine.

I pinch my lips together. "I will never—"

"Oh, Serenity, hush now. Even your mother doesn't have faith in your ability to resist me. Why would she be so adamant to take your place?" He inclines a hand to Serafina. "Chalk it up to maternal instinct all you want. I believe I am the only one who isn't pretending in this room. Have a good afternoon, ladies."

Triumph in his smoldering eyes, Force departs.

I purse my lips before confronting my mother. "Is he right? You don't trust me?"

"Serenity—"

"No." Holding up a hand, I survey her. "It's not just that. You trust her *more*, don't you? You're so scared I'm going to turn out like that monster?" I point to the door.

"It's not what you think." My mother walks toward me, then captures a few pieces of my hair. "There are parts of you I will never understand. I try not to let those parts concern me, but they do. I have no choice but to let them. It's something mothers do."

"You don't act like Bliss's mother."

My mother nods, assent in her creasing eyes. "She won't let me be her mother at this time. There is *something* between us. All I can do is nurture what little is there. I don't mean to push you away. Please try to understand."

I don't think I'll ever understand.

SKY

ONCE THE BEAST IS GONE—I can come up with much more colorful terminology, but I'll stick with that for now—Serenity rushes back up the stairs to meet me. I hear her footsteps on the marble. Smell her as soon as she opens the door.

Every time I see her, it gets harder.

But I'm still here whenever she needs me. Which is a lot. And that's fine with me.

Gesturing to the still-warm soup bowl on the nightstand, I grab it and start eating. Famished from my earlier excursion through the Temple rafters, I don't bother with a spoon. Just down all the contents of the bowl as quickly as I can. The action is not lost on Serenity.

Before she can say anything, I speak. "You know it's really not fair you get to enjoy all the fun stuff. Mouthing off to your father. Oh, and your suitors. I would've given my right arm to see the fork launch." I chuckle about the one suitor she told me about last night.

"But the fork didn't even stick," she whines. "Just bounced off his cheek. No, I think the night I dumped the ganache bowl over Director Vance's head was the best."

"The director from The Butterfly House?"

She chortles. "Now, he got a taste of what *my* butterflies can do that night."

I pause to smile down at my girl. She chews on her lower lip, and I try to avoid staring when she does. Try to avoid staring at her gorgeous, supple mouth.

"What have you been up to today?" she asks.

I shrug. "The usual. Spying on my brother, eavesdropping on your father, checking on Bliss."

Serenity's rodent in the rafters. The one fortunate thing about the Temple: the rafters between levels are generous. Of course they have security, but thanks to Kerrick's blueprints and my technological knowledge and Sanctuary gadgets, I've managed to stay under the radar. Getting in was planned months ago. Couldn't come in as security since Force interviews them all. Instead, I came in as a temporary employee. Forging a synthetic skin barcode was the difficult part. Hiring a double and transferring the skin was the easy part.

She treads on my last statement. "How is she?"

I put the bowl down. "Physically or emotionally?"

113

"Both."

I glance up at the ceiling and debate for a second. "Physically, she's holding up well, partly in thanks to your mother's healing. At night, she remains busy from what I can *hear*," I clarify to make sure she understands I'm not watching any of her private interactions. I don't stay for more than a minute or two. Part of me feels like lingering due to an almost-brotherly protection for Bliss, but she knows how to handle herself. Serenity does, too—just in a different way.

"What about Force or Luc?" she probes.

I give her the bare facts. "Luc is finalizing tonight's display. Your father has increased his security, which makes it more difficult for me. They haven't been able to determine where the murder took place or if it was a client or employee. Luc interrogated a suspect but concluded it was a dead end."

"So, what now?"

Should've figured she wouldn't let up. My persistent pest.

"Did you think it was going to happen overnight?"

She puts a hand on her hip, tilting her head to eye me. I mentally make a log of all the curse words I know. Doesn't she realize how adorable she is when she does that? Her questions used to climb all over me when she was little. Even though I know she wants to ask them, Serenity adopts this patient pose. It takes her some effort, but it lets me know how serious she is. She realizes I'm not telling her something. And she wants to know.

Dropping my arms to the sides, I shift my weight, conflicted about whether to tell her. Hope is a fragile thing in the Temple.

Damn. I swear she did that just to stab me. Folding her hands together into that prim pose. Terrific. If only I could find a way to master that mechanism. After all, she's held back on a few details herself. Something my brother undoubtedly pulled last week. Didn't need to be there. He's avoided me all this time, and when I've caught glimpses of his face through the vents, I can read the guilt there. He can't deny it even in private.

But she won't tell me, and I can't blame her. If I knew the details… but safety and caution are our ultimate priorities.

After watching her another moment or two, I drag a hand through my hair, ripping out its binding, and groan. "Fine, Ser.

You can cut it out now."

She just shrugs as if she doesn't understand, but I roll my eyes and finally relent.

"Force's fail safe...it could be anywhere inside Serafina. Even long gone from the Temple, he could activate it. Stop her heart whenever he wants. Only he can flip the off-switch to the implant."

She sighs, closing her eyes. Guess that's better than her face falling to the floor.

"When did you find out?"

"Yesterday."

She purses her lips. "Thank you for telling me."

"Hey." When I reach a hand out to stroke her cheek, I swear her skin gets softer every day. "Something you want to share?"

"Yes."

I pause. Gauge her expression. "But you're not going to, are you?"

"I can't predict how you'll react. If you could promise me—"

"If it comes to my brother, I can't," I tell her.

I've already come close to marching straight out of this room, grabbing him by the throat, and shaking the answer right out of him. But that would mean losing her, and she needs me more than ever right now.

"Best to leave it alone." I reassure her. "I have my theories, but if you confirm any of them for me, the results won't be pretty. If he wasn't too much of a coward to face me up here—"

"He doesn't fight fair. Like you."

"Hogwash!"

Turning around, I march toward the window before jamming the side of my arm up against it, leaning on it for support. I consider everything we've gone through. Sure, I've broken the rules, but not like him. Sure, I know her inside and out, and I've used that against her on an emotional level, but I don't operate on a physical one like him. That's just playing dirty, toying with her hormones. Luc has a superior sense of justification for it because I've known her all my life. He considers the playing field balanced.

But Serenity isn't a game to me. Never has been. And she knows that. Guess she always knew it, but it took Blackbird, the Shed, the lakeshore outside Neil's Museum, and my brother's own seductive idiocy for her to confirm it. I'll never forget the way she looked that night, her limbs trembling, skin shaking, cheeks flushed, body far warmer than it should've been. I was ready to beat him to a pulp. All it took was three words to stop me.

It's you, Sky.

I've always belonged to her. It was just the first night she belonged to me.

Serenity's arms fold around my waist, and I sigh before breathing her in and reciprocating. Doesn't get any easier, but I can deal with it. My conscience makes me. This damned Temple forbids me. And the knowledge Serafina would turn me into a shish kabob otherwise.

Twenty

MeRmaId

SERENITY

"STOP MOVING!" LINDY RAISES HER voice. "You are *so* fidgety."

"But I'm not moving at all," I protest.

Lindy dips her head and rolls her eyes. "I wasn't talking to you. Duh!" Then, she raises her hands and proceeds to scold her fingers. "I don't care if you haven't got any breaks today. Behave or I'll do that thing with the ice bath. Or we could try some of those horrid finger exercises again."

When her fingers pause from their trembling, she smiles. "Now, that's more like it."

I stifle a chuckle because then she'll just complain about *me* moving as she starts painting my skin again. More shimmer, more shine, but the prosthetic scales gliding up the sides of my legs feel so natural they could've grown there. Silver, naturally. Lindy's even applied a prosthetic finned ear with four points on each side of my head as well as gill prosthetics on my neck to complete the effect. The breathing implant was already grafted into my nostrils prior to the makeup application. A synthetic crystalline substance that absorbs all the oxygen in the room, transferring it to me—a miniature oxygen tank. Adding a gray-blue shade to areas of my skin helps to bring the underwater world onto my body. Grateful that silver scales flecked with pearls also coat my breasts, I feel more than eager to dive into my exhibit tonight.

"I'll apply your prosthetic fins shortly, but we'll do those closer to the tank. You'll be backstage, of course, so no one will see you."

"Do you know what he's planning?"

117

"Why would I?" Lindy straightens before arranging small portions of my hair into braids. "I'm just a preparer. I prepare you, not the exhibits. What a silly question. Wasn't that a silly question?" She laughs at her fingers.

"Can I see the tail prosthetic?"

Sighing, Lindy flicks a curl of my hair. "No."

"No?"

"No."

She doesn't provide a reason, and I shrug. A little too spontaneous about her work at times or maybe it's because she's busy and doesn't want the additional delay. I don't ask.

Once she's finished, Luc comes to escort us both.

He surveys the costume in full, and I try not to squirm as he does. I should be used to this by now, but the thought of Luc still using his artist's eyes on me are unsettling. Given what happened the other day, I wish my father would use someone else to bring the exhibits to life.

"Now, that's a siren if I ever saw one." Neil's voice interjecting immediately calms me down.

My half-brother kisses both of my cheeks, and Lindy smacks him. "What was that for?"

"You got *my* glitter all over your mouth now," Lindy points out. "No interfering with my makeup."

"You're just jealous cause I kissed her and not you." Neil winks.

"Of all the—" Lindy fumes as Neil leans over to goad her on. "Why I oughta—"

They continue their argumentative banter while I turn around to face Luc. "What's going to happen? What are you and my father planning?"

His hand advances toward my chin, but I recoil. Exhaling, he follows through with his habitual pattern and touches my shoulder instead. He pauses, taken back at the change. Guess I forgot all about the procedure. No more feather. It's a Yang symbol now. Nothing about the implant has changed, just the digital tattoo.

"You know I can't," he tells me, moving on from the symbol. "All I can do is offer you this—be the Serenity I've always seen."

"What the hell is that supposed to mean?" I hate it when he talks like that.

Neil raises his voice behind me, and I blow an annoyed breath because he and Lindy are still egging each other on. For once, my brother has met his match.

Luc dips his head to mine so he can murmur close to my ear. "Remember the night you told me about swimming in the ocean?"

I narrow my brows. My father wouldn't really—would he?

"Luc—"

"Look what you made me do!" Lindy half-screams. "We're late. Come on, Serenity. Ignore that pathetic waste of space."

"She calls me pathetic, yet she talks to her hands," Neil retorts.

"Shh…" Lindy coos to her fingers. "He's just not enlightened yet. He'll have to come back as multiple life forms before that ever happens."

As she ushers me out the door, I point a finger back to Neil, inviting him in a silent way to 'shut it'.

The three of us progress down a back hallway toward the exhibit, but instead of opening the door to the main room, Luc uses his barcode to gain access to a back stairwell. I wince just a little. What I do know about the murder was where the body was found. With both Luc and Neil behind us, I have little to worry about. Doing my best not to picture anything, I follow Lindy up the stairs, wondering if I'm leaving a glittery breadcrumb trail behind.

At the top of the stairwell are two doors side by side. Lindy takes the first one, which leads us to a small preparation area before the enormous tank. Considering the tank alone must have the surface area of a football field, I know the audience chairs must occupy a completely new level. This is a special exhibit detached from the main mermaid one.

A curtain divides the backstage area, but I can still hear the murmurs of an expectant audience. Lindy sets to work on applying my waterproof prosthetic tail while Luc and Neil observe. Her accomplished hands work quickly as she seals the edges of the tail around my shins where it greets the rest of the scales. Much different than what I expected—the tail is Lindy's shining spectacle. No wonder she didn't want me to see it first. Thin and transparent as a spiderweb, it's comprised of a network of parts all connected to the base of my legs, but the supple ends of the tail curl, reminding me of fine tendrils of hair. They move more like fabric.

"Now, that is really something," Neil admits before kneeling before Lindy. "My deepest apologies, my lady. I bow to your magisterial greatness!" The flirt takes her arm, then begins kissing the length of it.

Lindy eats it up. "It's about time someone appreciated my work."

I stare at the tail—or rather, the work of art—but there is no time. From some booming speaker around us, I can hear my father's voice welcoming the guests. The audience's applause roars in my ears.

"Here." Luc nudges a miniature speaker into my ear. "It's waterproof, and it will help."

Help with what?

"It's time."

I can't possibly stand. The tail restrains my feet far more than I care, but everything will be fine once I get into the water. Right now, I'm just trying not to shake and doing a poor job of it. I close my eyes for a moment, but that was a mistake. In the very next instant, Luc slides his arms around me and plucks my body up from the chair, entire ensemble included. The prosthetics must be heavy, but he handles me anyway. His arms remind me of the very first morning he'd held me—after he'd locked me above the client rooms.

"Shh." Luc tilts his head to mine as he tries to calm my quivering self.

He approaches one side of the tank where a small set of steps descends into the water. Kicking off his shoes, Luc approaches them with me still in his arms.

All the lights go dark. The audience claps again.

I bite my tongue. This never gets any easier.

Then, he kneels and lowers me into the water, voice murmuring in my ear, "Be Serenity."

Not the Swan, not a mermaid. Just Serenity.

Luc kisses me. In his twisted mind, maybe he thinks it will settle me, but his mouth printing against mine only spreads heat into my cheeks, yet causes me to shiver even more than the frigid saltwater. It stirs my lightning. The curtain still hasn't receded. I dive beneath the surface just as lyrical notes begin to play. From beneath the water, I still hear them from the speaker. Upon diving, the breathing implant in my nose triggers, harnessing its power. I don't have to hold my breath. It blocks any water and gives me oxygen, affording me an infinite supply of bubbles.

My suspicions are confirmed. I am in danger of loving this. While I buck against the notion, I know countless other girls only pretend to adore their time in the exhibits. Manipulation is key. Or belief, blind or otherwise.

I shouldn't waste the opportunity.

As soon as I begin to swim, the curtain lifts and spotlights encompass my form to unveil me. To get used to the sensation of my trapped legs and feet, I start swimming in small curls and circles, contorting my body this way and that. Spiraling my body backward is a thrill, somehow made simpler by the prosthetic tail that sweeps the water back and twirls to mimic my body's movements.

Then, I catch the shape out of the corner of my eye. A gray shadow. Just for a moment, but I pause from swimming and just float while my eyes narrow, focusing on the water paces ahead of me. A sense of foreboding creeps below my skin, and the haunting melody doesn't work to combat it. I see the shadow again, this time a little closer, close enough for me to make out its outline. Every drop of lightning freezes inside of me.

Oh yes, my father so would.

Be Serenity.

Closing my eyes, I inject my mind deep into the memory from my childhood. Of waves and salt and black water. Of a silver shape in that water.

What does this one smell? My fear? Does he notice the increase of my exhaled bubbles? Or can he hear my throat constrict?

I refuse to let my inner psyche be manipulated by a ridiculous terror.

Instead of recoiling in fear, I dare my senses, respect the shift of power, and swim toward the shark instead of away from it. Even with my mermaid-encrusted body, this majestic creature shames me. In fact, it pays little heed to another presence in the water. Respect fuses in my veins, bonding with my lightning to grant me the courage to pursue the water giant. Closer now, I reach out one hand and latch onto the top of its dorsal fin. Minding me no more than a tadpole, the shark continues swimming. For just a few seconds, he hauls me along. I get a sense of the powerhouse stored within its body. He's the one bestowing his beauty on me—not the other way around. He's not mindless or bloodthirsty.

Chilled to the bone, I withdraw my hand, let it glide along the sleek skin of his back before touching the tip of his tail as it flips back and forth. Then, I let go. The shark twists his body to the side, changing direction. Mirroring his movements from the side and careful not to invade his space, I swim along with him. I dance with him. The rows of countless teeth sharper than new arrow heads don't faze me at all. Not once does the shark open his jaws.

Intrigue, suspicion, and distrust breeds in the water between us. Sometimes, he avoids me. Other times, he approaches from the side, affording me the chance to sweep my fingers against his skin. Floating down deeper, I keep my movements subtle to honor his territory, working the lines of my body in simple curvatures and twists but no arcing gestures or backward flips. The shark rolls through the water nearby to investigate. My arms pirouette, and I tip my head back to him, the ends of my hair coiling up and tracing the side of his body. He circles and approaches, but he's not threatening. As the predator moves closer, I reach for him. The wide area of his nose bends, cupping my palm… but for just a moment because he doesn't linger.

Did a shark seriously just kiss my hand?

Hearing the familiar voice of my father on the speaker trespass on the very last notes of the song, I start to make my way up to the surface, pulsing through the water. Before I can reach the open air, a mechanical claw injects into the water and locks around my waist, plucking me from the tank like a piece of seaweed. The shock is so great I cough up water on my glide through the air right before the claw sets me down on a small, erected stage right before the tank where my father already stands.

Sliding one arm around my waist and raising a hand to the standing ovation of the crowd, he announces my mermaid name— Undine. They aren't specifically mermaids but more a class of water elementals that include everything from naiads to mermaids. I find it ironic since undines lack souls, unlike humans. Whatever the case, the applause increases, and my father turns to me and kisses my forehead.

"Well done."

LUC IS NOWHERE TO BE seen after the end of my exhibit. Guests disperse. I stand on the podium with my father until all have left, then Lindy arrives to remove my tail. I raise one brow when I notice Neil following her. When he produces a holographic device no bigger than a pinky nail, I realize he's getting some candid, behind-the-scenes footage. Perhaps to appease a curious audience who want to see what Undine is like in her off hours.

After Lindy frees my feet, I rise but discover how unsteady I am. Force catches hold of my arm to prevent me from stumbling.

"Steady, Serenity," he coos.

I suppose now is as good a time to ask as any. "I want to see the other exhibits again."

I'm not quite ready to leave the oceanic world yet.

"Check it out," Neil interjects, pointing to my sprite light views, which are going up by the thousands, comments spiraling. "You're a sensation! They're nicknaming you the Shark Whisperer."

Force grins, appreciative. "The mermaid exhibit room will be swamped with visitors, but I will take you to the back of the tanks if you wish to observe. You won't be able to see the girls as clearly, however."

Suits me fine. I'm not there to look at the girls. If I could, I'd spend all day in the water with the breathing implant even if it does prevent me from practicing my own ability to hold my air longer. Fortunately, it doesn't take too much time to remove it, but Lindy becomes frustrated at the technical assistant who must do so before she can strip the rest of the prosthetics from my skin.

Neil continues to get footage, but as Lindy's fingers work to peel away the scales near my thighs, I order him to get out.

"What? You know I've seen—"

Lindy turns on him, her blue eyes sharp as sea hooks, puckering up her plump, sugarplum nose. "Get out before I knock your block off, pretty boy!"

When Neil hesitates, Lindy goes so far as to push him toward the door.

"No farewell kiss?" he asks right before she shoves him out.

"I'd rather kiss the shark!"

She slams the door in his face, then shakes out herself. Her plump chest heaves up and down from the motion, and one side of her billowy blouse falls below her shoulder. Rolling it back up, she approaches me once more.

"Can you believe that twit?"

I stare down at her, noting the way her cheeks blush like honey bees have lodged there, stinging her repeatedly, willing blood to the surface. She blows aside strands of her short hair before smacking them away from her face and trying to concentrate on my legs. Quite attractive in her own way, Lindy has more than just her looks going for her. Sharp wit enough to take on my half-brother, a sweet sort of gumption, an eye for detail, and a face lovelier than a cherub. Make that a flushed cherub.

"You like him."

"What?" She pauses to glance up at me.

"My brother. You like him!"

She deadpans. "You know I could just *rip* off these scales."

Taking one corner of a scale right above my left thigh near my center, she tilts her head and waits for me to say something else. I know how much it would hurt. Better not to test her because I'd wager she'd follow through.

"I'll shut up."

"Good."

Lindy works her way up, easing her remover-coated brush under each scaly flap until I'm finally left with just my skin, which is still covered in glitter.

When she reaches for a washcloth, I hold up a hand. "Don't worry about the glitter. I'm sure Queran will remove it."

I change into a dress I discovered in my closet. Well, more like a closet within a closet for how large it is.

Lindy humphs a little, "Queran. I should have known he was your secret preparer."

"Jealous or something?" I wonder while slipping the dress on over my bra.

"He's a living legend in the Temple." She begins putting away her equipment. "Is it true he never talks?"

"Oh, he talks." *Just in a different way.*

I decide not to share his origami method of communication; it seems too intimate.

"So, about my brother…" I change the subject.

Lindy rolls her eyes. "Hey, I can still whack you with my brush," she threatens.

"What? You don't think he's a looker? You two actually have a lot in common."

"Yeah… like a leopard seal has a lot in common with a penguin."

I muse for a moment. "Are you the leopard seal?"

Lindy glares. "I've worked in the Temple long enough to have learned quite a few things. I know Neil is Nile Bodelo. He's spent his entire career globe-trotting and taking pictures of the most beautiful girls the world has ever seen. And I just prepare the girls so other eyes like his can feast on them. You wanna know what they call girls like us here in the Temple? Shadow girls. We're not meant to be seen or heard. Plain and simple."

"That's pretty cynical."

She shrugs. "It's the truth."

"Lindy." Approaching her with a smile, I cup her shoulder. "Trust me when I tell you this—my brother definitely sees *you.*"

MY FATHER DOESN'T HAVE MUCH respect for my privacy when we reach the back areas of the mermaid exhibit tanks. All I want to do is be alone with the water for a few minutes. After my swim, I feel light enough a cotton blossom could carry me away. This moment, this *aftermath,* is not his to share with me.

"Lovely dress. Pleased you have taken to your new wardrobe."

I glance down at the lady number, off-the-shoulder sleeves with silver filigree decorating it everywhere. In some ways, there is more filigree than fabric, which makes it heavier.

"More training tonight?" I spit out the words.

"Of a sort."

He doesn't provide me with any more information, leaving me suspicious with a gnawing sense of foreboding. What else could he have in mind for Bliss and me?

"She hasn't spoken to me all week, you know."

"It was expected. After all, you don't mix well."

"Yes, you saw to that."

"Not at all, my daughter."

Force watches me when I stop in front of a tank in the center of the exhibit. He's ruining this for me, but I try to focus on the way the exhibit lights capture the water like individual glowing smiles nestling inside the liquid ripples. For a few moments, I close my eyes and press my cheek against the glass to enjoy the silence before he interrupts it again. I wait, but my father says nothing. Curious, I open my eyes but see him at the end of the hall, exiting the exhibit room to give me some time alone.

Well, at least there's that.

I wander along the different tanks, discovering the back area is smaller than the front, half segregated from the opening of the main room and the hallway. Just as I approach the center tank again, I notice something white floating inside the tunnel holed into the underwater rock formations. Nearing the tank, I narrow my eyes to make out the white shape, hoping, praying, wishing it's not what I suspect. Corpse skin white as a December sky. I stare at her eyes, which remind me of peering past a fish's transparent scales into its exoskeleton. Through the space of the giant tank, I can hear the faded shouting protests and a scream or two from the crowd at the presence of a dead body in the tank. Some, no doubt, are running for the exits.

And I'm just frozen there. All I can do is gaze at the familiar mark sliced into her chest.

A swan.

Twenty-one
To ShAme

LUC

AT LEAST SHE ALLOWS ME to kiss her before I surrender her to the water. Small comfort, but I don't have time to consider it. Force gave me orders to inform Bliss of his plans for later. Ever since the Garden, I've stopped giving myself the luxury of watching Serenity's exhibits play out. Tonight will be grand, I'm certain. Indulgent coward I am, I know I will cave to the temptation of watching her feeds on my bed canopy tonight.

It takes some time to reach the Penthouse level to walk the halls to Bliss's room on the far side. Serenity will be a few minutes into her song now, but her father will draw this one out as far as he dares. Despite how well-trained the sea creature is and its programmed suppressor, the thought of her swimming with that beast unsettles me, which is why I must focus on the present and limit the images in my head.

I knock on Bliss's door.

No answer.

After my second knock, I use my barcode to open it just a crack. But she's nowhere in the main suite. Her bedroom door is wide open. Her father said she would be here. If he wasn't so preoccupied with ensuring everything was in order for Serenity's Undine unveiling, he would deliver the message himself. Not that I can blame the director after last week's unfortunate event—if it can be labeled that. He will go to extraordinary lengths to prevent another murder. Just as I would if I were playing director. As it is, I must buck from taking on that authoritative mold. At times, I've caught myself wanting to challenge Force, advise him on how to handle the situation. He welcomes my advice in certain areas, but Force is far more qualified at this position than I am. It is one area I can respect. Not his treatment of his daughters, but his treatment of the Temple—the precision in each one of his actions.

"Director Aldaine."

Bliss steps out from the bathroom, a wake of steam behind her. The white silk robe she wears holds her curves like a lullaby, outlining them. My eyes linger, exploring certain areas, deciphering differences in a matter of seconds. She is thinner than Serenity. Not as full in one singular area, but the contrast between the two of them is still quite subtle.

I turn to fix my gaze at a spot on the far wall. "Your father sent me with a message. I knocked twice, but there was no answer."

"I didn't hear you." She keeps her words simple and unadulterated. Unlike my roaming thoughts.

Bliss makes her way across the room and to her closet door, which is open. Less than a minute later, she returns with a white dress in her hand.

"How is Serenity's exhibit?" she questions me.

"Intense."

"I suppose it will stir an appetite for tonight's interaction." She stands before the mirror, tilts her neck to the side, and touches her fingers to her slender throat.

Her obvious attempt at small talk reminds me far too much of her father. I get to the point.

"A client has requested your services immediately following the interaction."

"And what business is it of yours?"

"None. Your father has merely tasked me with a message. He's planning to continue Serenity's training—inside your client room."

Bliss peers at me from her vanity mirror but only nods. "Thank you, Director Aldaine."

Shaking my head, I step toward her. "The Temple has only one director, and I am not him."

"My father says once a director, always a director."

"Not in my case. I rejected the title and my Family name."

She reaches an ornate box filled with a cream. "Do you have

another title you'd prefer to be known by?"

"Luc will suffice."

"Very well, Luc."

Bliss rubs the cream into the back of her neck, easing her hand underneath the robe. It slides back to give me a partial view of a week-old laceration there.

"Luc," Bliss says. "My personal preparer always takes time to rest before mine and Serenity's interaction together. I can summon a medic aid, but since you're already here, would you mind?"

She motions to the cream before sliding the edges of her robe down her shoulders to reveal the multitude of whip marks on her back. I consider refusing out of propriety's sake, but I am an artist first and foremost. Between that and my background as a director, I have seen countless girls, Serenity included. Bliss's body is familiar to me, but her skin feels altogether unique when I apply the cream to her scarred back. To her, there is nothing sensual about this moment. She doesn't close her eyes or lean her head to the side, and I can sense the rigidity in her spine. Bliss is trying desperately not to move, not to wince, cringe, or flinch from my fingers nursing the cream into the marks scattered across her skin. Some of the wounds betray signs of a skin fuser, others automatic grafting. But the healing cream laced with antiseptic is still a necessary process.

My eyes wander across the length of her back. Her bones protrude more than Serenity's, but it doesn't detract from her beauty. She reminds me of her father's glass sculptures. All delicate sharp angles. I'd give one hand just to sketch her.

The farther down I go, the straighter Bliss becomes. Finally, I pause, unable to withstand much more.

"Stop it." I gaze at her from the side.

Unconcerned over her exposure, Bliss angles her neck to ask, "What?"

I cup her chin. Unlike Serenity, she does not retreat when I tell her, "You don't have to pretend it doesn't hurt. I know it does. I've felt the marks myself."

"Expressing it won't change anything, will it?" she counters. "Pain is guaranteed. Suffering is optional."

"It makes one human. Something you seem to have forgotten,"

I accuse her.

"Hmm…" Bliss muses with a soft smile. "Your irony surprises me, Luc."

"Irony?"

"Yes, it's obvious you see no other girl in the universe but my sister. And yet, you're desperate to compare me to her. But perhaps I know why."

I place the cream box on the vanity, trying to ignore her. "I don't know what you mean."

Confronting her was a mistake. I should leave now.

"Please don't insult me." Bliss leans back in her chair, flaunting the two badges of honor on her chest, goading me on. "Anyone can see her rejection has trapped you. We both know Serenity will always get her way… just like Father does."

"*Stop.*" I'm in danger of raising my voice.

"But perhaps she really isn't lost, is she? After all, one identical body is as good as another."

The sheer force of her words, however softly she speaks, accosts me. A taunt dressed in silk.

"All this suitor business is just for Father's entertainment," she continues. "It's his way of playtime with her, of getting a rise out of her. Just as he manipulates you into believing you have a chance. No one has a chance. No one will ever be good enough for his little princess. But if your bed gets too cold one night—"

She starts to stand from her chair, ready to forsake the rest of the robe.

I turn my back to her. For the first time in all my years, I capitulate. I walk away from a battle with a woman, confirming her words at the same time. Serenity's warfare is far simpler than this. A physical level I can easily handle. Bliss prefers the psychological.

Screw Force.

His daughter puts him to shame.

Twenty-two
MoRe TraIning

SERENITY

"GO AWAY!" I FLING THE glass vase at my father's head as he marches toward me.

He swings his head to the side, evading my aim, and the glass shatters on the floor behind him. The determined smirk on his face reveals he's not daunted by my fit, however justified it is. Ever since I saw her corpse, ever since I saw the swan carved into her chest…it's only natural for fear to rise. For me, there is far more anger.

"As much as I'm enjoying your little tantrum, your interaction is at midnight, and I'm going to see you get to your preparation on time. Even if it means I have to drag you."

"Leave me *alone*," I scream, making a beeline for the stairs.

Force is taller than me, legs long enough to slice my stride in half. He grabs both my arms, thrusting them behind my back. "Come along, now. Your audience awaits."

I seethe. "How do you know one of them isn't a cold-blooded killer?"

"Two reasons. Number one, a killer with this sort of palette enjoys working his way up to the prize, and the savoring of that prize would only happen in private—not public. Number two, I am a cold-blooded killer myself, daughter. I can recognize one from a mile away."

Working his way up to the prize. That means more girls will have to die. More death…always death around me.

"You either come with me now or—" His words border on a

threatening promise. "I will make you watch while I whip your mother within an inch of her existence."

Oh no, he didn't! I weasel out of his grasp, hands primed for his throat, but my father grips onto my wrists and wrenches them apart, baring my face to his eye.

"My beautiful Swan. My little Skeleton Flower. My dark Undine." He samples on each one of my names. "No wonder you have a serial killer obsessed with you. No wonder every man in the world would deal with the devil himself just to bed you. You're already sending my Temple climbing to the edges of the galaxy!"

I spit in his face. "Before it dives straight down to hell."

Force leans in to murmur. "Let's go together, shall we?"

AFTER THE BURNING ENCOUNTER WITH my father, Queran's hands feel like water on my skin. His words, soft as silkworms, soothe my quaking nerves. And the origami mermaid holding onto a shark made me smile.

While Queran prepared Bliss, I took the moments to come down off my dark horse, but the lightning is still warming my blood. Free to walk around in her Yin skin—nothing new unlike all my Temple Face costumes—my sister reflects on my fury, which could have melted her bedroom floor more than my pacing feet wore them down.

Tonight, our interaction style is different. While Bliss is still the dark one, her Yin skin is more of a midnight blue rather than black and provides a sharp contrast to the fiery gold Queran paints on mine. Gold flecks and glitter complement the paint. Queran even attaches a whimsical gold skirt to the backs of my legs. Full-bodied complete with ruffles. On the contrary, Bliss's skirt is a spill of blue ink.

"Father thinks you should be flattered," she dictates as she paces.

"Excuse me?"

"He takes a sense of pride. A serial killer has chosen you as his inspiration vessel. It will only bring more repute to the Temple. It will go down in history."

I can't believe she just said that! I slam my fist down on the table, but all that does is upset all the makeup tools there. An overly concerned Queran scrambles to my front and touches his fingers to my cheeks, staring into my eyes.

"Shh, sweet girl!" His fierce whisper competes with the softness of his fairy wing-blue eyes.

I lick my lips and nod, accepting the way his forehead brushes mine. "Yes, Queran, yes."

I take a few moments while he rights the objects on the dresser, arranging them again by height and purpose. Sucking in a deep breath as he continues to paint my arms, I prepare to confront Bliss.

"Killing girls is not a compliment," I tell her, feeling like a scolding teacher just for having to tell her this. "It's murder. It's wrong."

"In some cases, yes."

I shake my head. "In *all* cases. You're destroying a soul, plain and simple."

"Souls are a fickle thing in the Temple. We are not all innocent. Girls lose theirs much too fast here."

"Like you lost yours?" I flick my head to her.

Bliss does not respond.

Queran takes his time, brush smearing paint around my elbow. Careful and conscientious.

"I didn't lose mine," my sister finally says after a few minutes.

"Do you just deny it? Bury it so deep you don't even know what it feels like anymore? Do you feel *anything* anymore?"

Even in Yin's dark skin, Bliss doesn't seem real. If I could see her soul, I imagine it would look like a frozen bubble. Maybe my father keeps it locked up somewhere. Maybe he keeps the soul of every girl locked in glass jars in his Temple somewhere. He must take them out and look at them every day, pleasuring himself with their temporary satisfaction.

Not mine. He'll never get a hold of my soul.

We spend the rest of the time in silence, barely looking at one another. Queran is ready to paint my front, and I drop my robe. He pauses to raise a finger, and I've grown familiar with the action. After all, he spent an hour just painting my whole back. He needs another bathroom break.

Several times, I turn to eye Bliss, but she doesn't reciprocate. It doesn't matter. I force myself to meet her eyes because of what will ultimately come later. It has to mean something to her. It means something to me—the way she doesn't just suck our father's poison into herself, she's part of it. Like her body is trapped in the poison bottle, skin washed in it all the way up to her neck. Just a pocket of air at the top to give her breath. But it's enough for her.

How can she breathe so freely when I feel like I'm suffocating?

And then, I consider…if her soul is a frozen bubble, it's unbreakable. Because she won't let herself break.

IT FEELS LIKE I'M A rock—weighed down and strapped to this table—with an overdose of moss smothering my face.

"Yes, she seems quite feisty tonight."

"Not her sister. So stoic."

I crane my head to see the speaking gentleman trace a finger along the swell of Bliss's breast. No, not gentleman. There's nothing gentlemanly about any of them. One by one, I pick them off, eyes impaling them. The only one they can't pierce is my father.

"Stoic is old hat," one closer to me mentions, plucking up a small bead of salmon roe from my navel. "A girl with some fight appeals to a more refined palette."

"Cause you're *so* refined, Wallace. What was then name of that two-bit Breakable stripper in Club Wonk last weekend?"

"Sod off, James."

Everyone at the table jumps at the sudden sound of a gunshot cracking the interaction in half. All my nerve wires pop like buttons. Butterflies scramble about in my stomach, some flying for cover, others flapping their wings and muttering curses, still others rearing their heads, shaking wild antennae. I twist my head to the side to see two gunmen entering the room. Masked, of course. How on earth had they gotten weapons into the Temple? They knock out the security guard they smuggled to get up to the Penthouse. Only the highest dorm levels require my father's interface. Not the conference level.

"Don't move! None of you move," they bellow out the orders.

"Don't try anything!"

Are you kidding me right now?

One of them gets the message too late. The other men shout in protest when their comrade ends up shot and slumped on the floor. I can't tell whether he's dead or alive. Too much is happening. I don't know whether to look at my sister or my father, but I end up settling on my father. If anyone in the Temple has a gun, it would be him. Then again, my father's cutthroat sense does prefer knives. One of the gunmen keeps his weapon primed on Force while the other approaches the table.

"Ladies and gentlemen, thank you for your cooperation," one of the masked gunmen sarcastically states. "We are here for one thing and one thing only. Miss. Yang?"

I flick my head toward the gunman, face a mask.

"If you'd be so kind…" He gestures for me to get off the table.

What a day I'm having. My shark was more well-behaved than this.

Sushi tumbles off me as I start to get up. First, I glance at my sister, who hasn't moved whatsoever, then at my father, who clenches the balcony railing so hard his knuckles turn white. But he'll bleed that railing long before a blood drop leaves his body. I couldn't care less if any of the men here gets shot. If my father didn't have that damned implant, I wouldn't care about him, either.

"Very good," the gunman commends me. "Now, walk to the elevator. The three of us are going to take a little *ride* together."

By the way he says "ride," I know full well what he's referring to. Biting the inside of my lip, I start toward them slowly, delaying as long as possible.

"You are making an enormous mistake, gentlemen," my father states from his balcony perch.

I'm at the right angle to see the elevator doors sliding open once more, but the assailants can't, and they don't hear the elevator opening.

"And who's going to stop us, Director? You?"

I pick up where my father left off. "No, you should really worry about *him*."

Neither man gets a chance to turn before Luc seizes both their guns, dismantling them within seconds. It doesn't stop one from grabbing me, dragging me back and forcing a knife against my throat. Too hard. I feel a nick there. Luc forces his partner to his knees, fracturing his arm, earning a howl from the man just before smashing his head against the glass floor. Luc rises to confront the one holding me.

"Mmm," the masked man murmurs in my ear. "Worth it just to touch you, Swan."

"That's not my name," I declare, my voice bone-needle sharp.

My father starts to descend the staircase. "Release my daughter immediately. You're going to die no matter the case. It's up to you whether your death is slow or instantaneous."

"As I see it, I still have the upper hand." Sarcastic again, he raises one gloved hand before smoothing it up along my stomach, moving higher.

My father throws a blade, which whistles through the air and finds its mark in the man's hand. His scream reverberates in my ears at the same time as the assailant's knife clatters to the floor. I dive right out of his arms but bring one leg up to kick him in the stomach. It reminds me of the time I kicked the auctioneer. Not quite as satisfying, but my father has his moment when he arrives and grabs the blade handle to tug, arresting another scream from the man's mouth. Finally, he removes the mask, flinging it to the floor.

"Well, now. One of my very own security members, I suppose knocking out Donner was just a ruse to avoid suspicion. What exactly were your plans, Rockwall? I'm extremely interested."

Rockwall is on his knees now, gripping his shoulder. "Screw you! You should've known this would happen, parading her around, dangling her in front of our faces, knowing no man on a guard's salary could ever afford her, but we're still supposed to protect her? Screw you!" He spits in Force's face.

He's no longer my father in this moment. Once more, he is Syndicate. His next blade cut is for the security guard's neck. Tit for tat for what he did to me. More slices follow…in various places. Force circles Rocky, meandering around with a sick smile, monster in the seams.

Compared to my father, my shark is a pussycat. The next gash

136

is on Rocky's back, which causes him to double over in pain. Force is demonstrating his power and position in the Temple, showing the men all around him what happens when someone tries to steal from him. Their gazes are rooted on the display, most donning approving smiles but with squeamish-pale cheeks.

"Serenity…" Luc urges me away from the sight, wrapping me in his coat, anchoring me close to his side. I look back. "My sister—"

"Your sister is fine. Come with me."

Fine.

There she is on the table—not having moved at all, eyes still closed. Tranquil as—as a swan. She puts me to shame.

Because Bliss is always fine. And I envy her for that.

My father is a real piece of work.

The client sits in a luxurious chair, a duplicate copy of my father's. At least I'm allowed to wear whatever I want for training, which is my usual clothing. Not Bliss. When I enter the room, wearing a fresh dress, she is kneeling with her head bowed low to the ground, the roll of vertebrae almost cutting through her thin back.

She is topless for him. Only dressed in a pair of thigh-high satin stockings, white and transparent, little bows tied at the top.

"Good evening, Serenity. I trust there are no hard feelings about last time," Drake comments as he puffs his fine-crafted cigar.

Everything my father does is an act. Even when he pretends to defend me. Drake reminds me of a werewolf with the thick dark beard he sports and hooded eyes beneath shadow-imparting brows. His clothes—or lack thereof—since he remains shirtless as if he's proud to display the grandeur of his *under*developed muscles—suggest a casual indifference.

Wrath spikes within me over the events of the past few days. Maybe Force even plotted the attempted abduction to create more stress. In my mind, I conjure up all sorts of colorful torture for him. But the whip is in my hand, and Bliss is at my feet—waiting.

That's when I notice the laser projection behind Force and Drake. Force must notice because he gestures and states, "Doc-

137

umented today so I may view it later and determine where any errors take place. But I will send the appropriate feeds to Drake later."

How many feeds have been made of Bliss? I can't fathom. My feeds are now global, but they are solely of my exhibits. Not this… hell.

I turn to my father, so desperate to use the whip on him. He pats his chest in silent reminder. *Beat, beat. Beat, beat.* Serafina's heart beats with his. If that wasn't enough, the electric baton he carts with him for training is a stinging reminder he is still in control.

I raise the whip.

And strike.

I bring it down on Bliss's skin harder than I meant to because it separates an older wound with no effort.

Now, I feel it. I loathe it. I loathe myself even more for not stopping it, for letting *it* bite my butterflies. There's no excuse for letting the monster out. Whatever has happened—Kerrick's murder, my mother's heart numbing, Bliss's own iciness, Luc's persistence with me, exhibit pressure, a serial killer marking his symbol onto his victims, interactions, my father—none of these give me permission to unleash this monster. Oh, it feels entitled. It tells me that striking the whip against my sister's back is a coping mechanism—a way of releasing all the tension and stress of the Temple. Like I'm transferring it from my blood to hers, but does it even sink in or does it just drip down her skin?

In the middle of the process, after I've scored more of her back than the first time, Bliss doesn't cry. And when she smiles even when she's doubled over with blood trickling down her back, I strike one last time. As soon as she seizes, spasms, and passes out, I sink to the floor, clutching handfuls of my hair, still holding the whip.

Glancing down, I notice I've torn my dress sleeve. A second later, the smart fabric repairs itself, sewing the tear closed until there is no trace of any rip. If only inner healing could come that easily.

"Give her a moment," I hear my father tell Drake.

"This more than makes up for last weekend's event, Director. I

138

am extremely impressed."

"Yes, it was a necessary device, you understand."

"Most assuredly," Drake says. "This event has proved quite intoxicating. I'll look forward to replaying the sprite light as the young ones call them now. You should be proud."

"I am."

"Bliss is a fine morsel indeed, but it'd still be a thrill to sample your other daughter. Especially given what she is," he says, referring to my virginity.

"Hmm…" My father chuckles. "It would be a cold day in hell, my friend. Unlike my other daughter, Serenity is far too priceless for you. She is more interested in a long-term engagement. The man for her must be singular indeed, but you are free to ask."

"Well, then." Drake sets aside his wineglass and rises. "Interested, Serenity?"

I grit my teeth, twisting my head slowly toward them, rousing the monster into my eyes before crouching and cracking the whip in their direction. My father just beams when it flies within an inch of Drake's body. Then, Force extinguishes his cigar in the same moment I get to my feet.

"You may want to depart now, Drake. Otherwise, I cannot be responsible for my daughter's actions. She and I are remarkably similar, you understand. As soon as production of the feeds are finished, they will be sent."

"Thank you for a splendid evening, Director."

They shake hands as I approach. When Drake turns to thank me, I crack the whip again. This time it lands, cutting into his sleeve, drawing just a hint of blood. Drake winces but still departs.

Force alerts a medic for Bliss, but I start to leave before the aid arrives. My father seizes me by the arm, and I grit my teeth and raise the whip, growling, threatening.

"You can't hide from your own father," he confronts me in a stalemate. Neither of us is prepared to back down. "I know what you were feeling tonight."

I pinch my eyes together. "You think *this* helps? It makes it all worse!" I tighten my grip on the handle.

My father touches the back of my hand and tilts his head to the side, peering at me like an owl would. "Then, why do you want to use it more than ever?"

I drop it. Drop it all. Clenching my eyes, I try to get a hold of my emotions, but my father won't let me go. This time, he lets me strike him. Gratified by the sight of my nails stripping the flesh off his cheek, I pursue him, pushing him, shoving him back and back until he hits the wall, knocking over the table with the wine in the process. He's up against the wall now. With the lightning monster inside me feeding, I raise my fist until I find him laughing, cackling maniacally, and that's when my eyes take stock of the situation. All my butterflies crash against the monster like a tsunami. Enough to force it back under. Fist crumbles, fingers break apart so I can see gaps between them again.

I almost stumble back, but my father takes me by the waist, then frames both sides of my head to pull me close to his chest.

"My beautiful, beloved daughter."

Then, he cups my cheeks and tilts my face up to meet his. One feather-light touch of his lips against mine. He strokes the side of my face and then holds me again.

"Shh…"

His fingers feel like fire on my back. On my cheek, his breath is burning rope. I have to get away.

This time, he lets me escape. I run from him. Run from Bliss. I run from it all, but I'm still not free. I crash right into Luc—the last person I want to see, the person I loathe as much as my father.

"Let me go," I hiss, trying to wrestle from his arms.

He grips my wrists, preventing me, pushing me too hard. "Stay with me, Serenity."

He's asking for more than just my physical presence. He understands what happened in that room. My eyes hold enough for a book.

Luc leans in to kiss me, but I break free and scream, "Oh, leave me alone for once in your life!"

Twenty-two

ToO LaTe

BLISS

THIS IS MY PUNISHMENT. FOR everything I am. The unchosen twin. The pain reminds me I shouldn't have been born. That I was broken right from the womb. It's why I've never been able to please him.

Only she can.

How could she ask if I lost my soul when I didn't possess one in the first place? If I ever had, it hadn't survived childhood. If it still exists, Father must play with it daily, wondering if it will come to life.

Again and again, my body seizes. It's beyond a level I can manage, but I still try. I don't permit my mind to engage in an ice bath—one of my coping mechanisms. Her attacks have more force now. Out of the corner of my eye, I catch one glimpse of her. Her eyes seem to get brighter each day—tinted by Father's growing fire. Tonight, she's welcoming it instead of pushing it back. She's feeding the beast inside her. It won't be long until Father turns her into exactly what he wants her to be.

Still, I remember to smile.

The blows are closer together now, more insistence in their strikes. Each one is more potent than the last. I want to whimper. By the end, I've bitten my tongue to prevent myself from screaming. I taste blood. My entire body is a pattern of scars all joined together to create one. An unworthy blot on the universe. A stain on a glass floor that can never be scrubbed out.

Serenity is the apple of Father's eye. She is the apple at the very top of the tree—the kind men will climb over each other to get. I am the bruised and rotted apple on the ground. Full of maggots and worms that feed on the leftover pieces over and over because that is what men do. All they ever will do.

Twenty-three

ImpOssIble to FiNd

SKY

THIS IS WHERE SHE FEELS safe.

I shake my head, smirking at the irony, but I give her the time and space she needs. Just observe for now. It doesn't take a genius to figure out why she's here. After I witnessed the aftermath in the hall with Luc, I was ready to drop to the ground then and there and knock him out for grabbing my girl. He's still too much of an idiot to understand that when she's breaking down, the last thing she needs is someone grabbing her like that.

Sometimes, the best way is to let her get back up again on her own.

Her hands are shaking. I can see it from where I hide at the very back of the audience chairs, concealed in the shadows. In the darkness, her white space sticks out. She's like a statue of lace. Lace that's tearing. And this is how she copes.

Normal girls have puppies or kittens. My girl has a shark.

I saw her footage live on her lower-level suite screen. It was easy, knowing her father wouldn't interrupt me. Too close a call. I even got into the hallway with the full intent of marching into the exhibit room, diving into the water, and taking on the shark—two hundred and forty teeth and all since I'm counting the developing ones. But the song was still playing in the background, so I chanced a glance back, and there she was. Swimming *toward* the thing!

My impossible girl.

I sat and watched every last agonizing minute.

My smile grows when I overhear her speaking to it. I'm sure she'd cope better in the water, but she respects the predator's privacy. They're still getting acquainted after all.

I watch as the shark sweeps past her, and she traces her hand against the glass of the tank, following him.

"You know what it feels like, don't you, big boy?" Her words are farther away, but I still hear them. "You're not trying to be a monster. Certain people, circumstances can bring out the worst in you. You're built for it. Like it's fate, ingrained into your DNA, but that still doesn't give you a right to bite peoples' heads off, does it?"

She presses her hand to the glass, angling her head to the shark. Since I manipulated the cameras in the exhibit room, I can make my way down. But she's working her way back up from her knees, so to speak. So, I give her a little more time to work out her own thoughts.

"Maybe it gives you a reason, an explanation, but it doesn't make it right. But what do you do? What are you supposed to do when the blood is dangling right in front of you? When she just... lets you? When someone will get hurt no matter what. It feels so impossible."

"It's not impossible, Ser."

"Sky?" She turns to me, surprise registering, but she doesn't run to me even if I'm still on the stairs a good few paces away.

She's not quite ready yet. So, I keep things light enough for her.

Stuffing my hands in my pockets, I stroll down the concrete steps to join her by the tank. "Nice shark. What are you gonna name him?"

"Why? Did you have something in mind?" She smiles.

Good.

"Shouldn't ask me." I shrug. "You know I'm not good with names. All I can come up with is something stupid like Jaws."

"That is really stupid," she banters.

Better.

"I was thinking something more fitting. Like Sharky."

"Hmm..." Crossing my arms over my chest, I study the Great White. "Works for me."

I press a hand to the glass. She does the same. Starts to inch it little by little to mine. I don't move. I let her come to me. She tugs on my sleeve, harder. That's when my arms come around her. When I surround her. The back of her head sinks onto my chest, and her arms crisscross over her chest to welcome mine folding over them. I cave, bringing her down with me so she can feel free to crumble into me.

Sharky sweeps past us, tail swinging toward her.

I tilt my head down. Press my mouth to the side of her head. "I think he misses you."

My mouth finds her cheek, tasting salt there. Leftover from sweat or from her swim, it's difficult to tell. Either way, she smells and tastes like my Serenity.

"What if *you* miss me?"

It's not difficult to read between the lines with her. "You've got more fight in your pinky than most girls have in their whole body. You got me backing you. You got your mother's love. You got Kerrick's raising. And we got heaven smiling down on us."

"How do you know?"

I nudge her so she will look up at me. Need her to understand that some things in life can never be accidents. Her and me? We're not an accident.

"Because I wasn't supposed to be there that day." I kiss the tip of her adorable nose. "I wasn't supposed to be on that floor, in that hall, or by that elevator. No lucky stars or coincidences, Ser. That was too big a moment to leave to chance. Someone out there's looking out for us. I told you we can beat this world."

"What if I can't beat myself?"

"You can."

"How do you know?"

"I just know."

Straightforward.

"That's a lousy answer. Like when you used to tell me 'because I said so'. I never listened. I need a reason."

On the verge of grumbling, I somehow muster up a simple sigh and try to figure out the right words. "Hold onto your passion. Hold onto your love. You hold onto your magic, Ser. Never let it go. I'll hold onto my faith. Simple as that."

Between the facts, the reasoning, the plans and processing, and my brain firing a million miles a second, faith is what keeps me sane.

"Nothing's felt too magical lately," she says.

"I beg to differ!" Giving her a little poke, I nod toward the tank where Sharky swims past us.

Finally! It's about time I roused a giggle out of her. It must multiply inside her because she throws her head back against my chest—full-blown laughter. I chuckle. That's my crazy, cockamamie girl. I inhale the scent of her hair all around me. Perfume practically drowns all the strands, but if she doesn't care, I don't either. Serenity could smell like a dung beetle, and I'd still want to kiss her senseless.

"Come here whenever you need to," I tell her, gesturing to the tank.

She cranes her head to see me. "Is this our *waterfall*, Sky?" she asks, referencing our meeting place in the Aviary.

I grin. "It's better."

"Almost."

I know that look in her eye. The one she gets right before she closes her eyes and starts to lean up to me. I meet her. Unless she's just gorged herself on chocolate, Serenity's never tasted sweet. Nevertheless, she's exactly right for me. Her mouth reminds me of our times in the water together—all depth and memories, few clothes but many secrets. That's what I want for the rest of our lives.

"Only one thing's impossible," I murmur against her mouth.

I need this break, this little gap to remind myself of my own humanity—before I do something I'm gonna regret.

"Huh?" Her breathless voice asks.

"You. You're impossible. But you're *my* impossible."

She brings her shoulders together with a smile. "That doesn't make any sense."

I shake my head. "Sounded better in my mind. But I'll tell you this—" I pause to sift my hands in her hair, cup them around the back of her neck because she doesn't like them hanging around her face. "You're an impossible girl to find. Except for me. I'll always find you. Just like the day you were born."

"Funny, I thought I found you."

I plant both my hands in hers and kiss her forehead, hoping she takes the hint I've got to stop for a while. "We found each other."

As soon as I hear the door open on the other side of the exhibit room, I hurry away from her and rush as fast as I can behind the auditorium-like chairs.

SERENITY

WHEN MY FATHER ENTERS THE exhibit room, I don't move. I don't take the risk of my father thinking I wasn't alone by me looking back even for a second. Instead, I focus on Sharky and sidle up against the tank.

Every time Force gets close to me, my world feels like it shrinks to the size of a teacup. Chance of escape is minuscule at best. How long before my father steeps me with his boiling water, drains my flavor to use it to his satisfaction, and dries me out?

"I thought it would be best to check on you." He approaches me with the same body language I've grown accustomed to: hands folded behind his back, slight hunch, tilted head with an edge of insanity in his eyes.

I don't answer. Tonight, I give him nothing.

And when I walk away without a confrontation even after he grabs my arm, I make sure he knows it.

When I take the elevator, it's up to her floor on the other side of the Penthouse. What I don't expect is to find my mother instead of Queran inside her bedroom. Not to mention Luc. However, he's on his way out the door, and though it surprises me that he doesn't meet my gaze, I welcome his lack of attention. I turn mine to my sister.

Her eyes are closed, but I can still see her trying to defy the instinctive wincing when my mother starts to apply antiseptic. Chancing a nervous glance, I expect to see lake-wide gashes. Instead, most of the wounds have fused together and grafted. The skin fuser rests on a nearby table—a newer model than Jade's.

My mother has already cleaned the blood away.

At first, I stand in the corner of the room until my mother motions me to come forward. To finish what she has started. This is the first time the three of us have been together since the Breakable

Room.

"My girls."

My mother speaks the two words—softer than snowfalls—and touches us in separate ways. While she feels comfortable fiddling with my curls, she reserves her hand to a simple touch on Bliss's shoulder that lasts only a moment.

"You might think you have nothing in common but your DNA, but you have the most important thing—me." She looks back and forth between us. "I hope, I pray, you can at least hold onto that."

When my mother leaves the room to give us some time alone, she takes her words with her. They disappear like a puff of smoke from a storybook dragon. Bliss doesn't open her eyes.

My hands aren't slow when I pick up the antiseptic bottle. My fingers aren't thoughtful. They seem to register how much this is going to hurt—us both. But it's necessary.

"Serenity, I don't want—"

"Shut up," I interrupt her, and she's not in much position to move. "I'm doing this whether you like it or not. Our mother's right. Deny it all you want, but we both made our choices because of her. I've got to deal with that same as you. You might like keeping walls between us, but I'm going to keep wrecking them over and over again. If the past seventeen years won't stop me, this sure as hell won't either." I spread the ointment onto her back, and I don't recoil when my fingertips find the healed but raised flesh wounds—wounds I created.

After a few minutes of Bliss cringing and gasping through the pain of the cream, she finally tells me, "I didn't have a choice."

"Neither of us did," I reply, thinking of our birth written in Mom's journal.

"Luck of the draw." Her voice doesn't sound convincing.

I shake my head, picking up on the frailty of her words. "No, it was *her* choice. She couldn't keep on forever. No one can. No one should."

"I manage. You won't."

My hand pauses. "That's what this is all about, isn't it? That I'll turn into him. This is really the worst barrier between us? Worse than seventeen years?" I touch one of the wounds.

"Your blows feel just like his."

Bliss doesn't look at me.

Inhaling deep, I blow out a long string of breaths and confess, "You're right, Bliss. Something deep inside me wants to accept the power. I'm not immune to our father's poison. I was overdosing on it while you're on the receiving end, which is worse…I know it is. But—" I lean over, pressing my cheek to the pillow next to her until I can see her eyes. "I've got something stronger inside me. I didn't put it there; it was always there. Sometimes, we take the good with the bad. If I believed there was no hope, I could never look into your eyes again, but I am right now."

I pause in case she responds, but she doesn't. She just stares back. For the first time, she's looking at me and not through me.

"Call it love, call it hope, call it whatever you want," I go on. "But it's more. Those things can fade. What I have lasts forever. And that's truth. I'm not ready to give that up."

I scoot closer. Nothing in my body speaks of comfort because this is not a moment for comfort. Not surprised she doesn't move even when I kiss her cheek. Bliss remains perfectly still like a ship in a bottle. I can't get her out unless I break the glass. Whether I've created a hairline fracture, I can't begin to imagine. I kiss her other cheek, but I can't will her to accept them. She has to do that on her own.

"I'm not a good person, Bliss. I'm just human. And this human has some good in her she won't let go."

BLISS

THE MOUNTAIN OF BROKEN BODY parts inside me is not doing its job. It's supposed to protect me from this, hold back the emotions, keep me numb. She thinks the stripes on my back are what divides us. She thinks the seventeen years without a sister are the problem. No, those can be overcome, chalked up to the fault of others. What can't be overcome is the time we were at our closest—a time frame of all of nine months.

History repeats itself. I suck the punishment into myself just as I did then. Broken before birth so my sister could be whole.

I'm an egg. Someone cracked me open before I was fully formed, poured out my golden treasure, and scrambled me up. I can't be unscrambled. But my sister still has a chance. I understand that now. She might be cracked, but she could get the chance to hatch before my father defines what she will become, before it's too late. It will be better for all of us if she and Serafina leave.

"There is a certain drug they keep in the Centre supply level," I tell her, flinching when her fingers descend on my back again. "It counteracts Father's implant. Use it, take Mother, and go."

"Not without you."

"Serenity—"

"Oh, I want to slap you right now, so just—don't say another word. I'm not leaving without you. Do you think Mom ever would? We won't leave without you."

"This is my home," I deny without moving. "It's all I've ever known."

"*We* are your home."

I try something else. "And what about Luc?"

"Don't change the subject."

I should've known she would see through my ploy.

"Like you said," I tell her with a sigh. "I am part of the poison. But it's my choice now. I am who I am."

"You can change."

"I am who I was made to be."

I wouldn't know what to do outside the Temple. She has to see that. She has to understand that even if she were to drug me and carry me out of its glass walls, I would go running back to them as soon as I could. As far as I'm concerned, the world outside the Temple doesn't exist. It's no better than here. At least I have access to everything I need. Plus, Serenity's Sanctuary would never accept me. If she knew who I really was, Serenity would never accept me either.

"Give yourself a chance to see someone different," Serenity urges while pulling out something from her skirt pocket—a small, leather-bound book. "It's Mom's journal." She sets it on the pillow next to me, treating it like a precious gift the way her fingertips linger on its cover. "She's a good writer. She talks about everything. Leaving the Temple, raising me, loving Kerrick, rescuing girls and getting them to the Sanctuary..."

I can't be saved, and I don't want to be rescued, I want to tell her, but she's in no position to hear it or comprehend.

"She'd want you to read it, too."

Serenity finishes applying bandages to my back, then stands up to leave me alone.

"I love you, Bliss," she stops to tell me before she reaches the door. "Whether you accept it or not, I'm going to love you."

I don't tell her how many times I've heard those words. They sound different coming from her mouth, but I know that's just a trick. True love can't exist in the Temple. She's too innocent to grasp that, but if she doesn't get out of here soon, Father will force it down her throat.

Hearing another door click from the other side of the room, I don't bother to glance over at him. Queran is always concerned over my physical welfare after these occurrences. He's coming to check the healing measures have been applied correctly.

"How long were you eavesdropping?" I smile at him as he sinks onto the bed.

Queran returns the smile and shrugs.

"Naughty, naughty," I scold him a little.

Then, he reaches for the paper object he formed for me long ago on the day we first met. I keep it hanging from my bed as a helpful reminder of what survival in the Temple should feel like. Leave the beauty; chuck the heart. Managing to prop myself up on my elbow, I lean onto my side to face Queran, careful not to disturb the bandages on my back.

My preparer twists his other hand in a magic trick to make a small origami heart appear. Slowly, he inches it toward the tetrahedra and injects it inside the complex network of triangles until it lodges in the center. It doesn't look right to me. Like all the intersecting triangles are suffocating it.

Then, he presses his hand to the space between my breasts where my heart lies. "Beat, beat," he whispers, but then wags a finger back and forth, shaking his head—it's not beating yet.

"It doesn't beat because there's nothing there," I deny.

Queran shakes his head again, pointing to the paper heart and then back to my chest.

I shrug. "Whatever you say, Queran."

Twenty-four
SeRafina's QuesTions

LUC

*F*ROM A DISTANCE, I WATCH my brother. I watch how he handles her. Why is he waiting? It doesn't take a genius to know he wants to talk to her, to hold her. I contrast our backgrounds, chalk it up to raising. That raising still defines me; I will never shirk it off completely. I gave up everything for her, and she'd rather talk to a shark than endure two words with me.

What are you waiting for, Skylar?

After what seems an eternity, my brother makes his way down toward her. Still, I can't fathom why he pursues her at this agonizing pace. Instead, he waits for her to raise her hand, to pursue him. As I leave, every phrase my father reared me with haunts me.

You want to be a real man, Luc? Don't wait for any woman.

She belongs to you, so just take her.

The world is your oyster. You have the right to as many girls as you desire. That is what being a man is all about.

Don't forget, a better one's just waiting over the next horizon.

Every woman secretly wants to be dominated.

And the world told me the same.

"Just give her some time, Aldaine," Force advises me. "She'll come around."

I'm sure, I mutter internally, tone sarcastic. Without bothering to acknowledge him, I continue on my way, intending on returning to my room, careless if he discovers my brother at the tank. Sky is too cautious for that. Sketching will grant me peace of mind, and since the last exhibition is complete, it's time to set

152

the stage for her next one.

Force keeps pace with me.

"Wait just a moment."

Pausing, I incline my head toward him.

"On your way back, would you mind helping get Bliss back to her room? It seems she passed out after her last client appointment. Her medic should be arriving in her room at any moment to test her blood and vitals. Thank you." He doesn't wait for my answer.

I roll my eyes, knowing he has countless security guards who could do this for him. Perhaps he is being extra cautious with his Yin and Yang due to the earlier incident with security. Whatever the case, Bliss's unconsciousness puts me at ease. After our last encounter, I have no wish to speak to her, much less listen to anything she might say. All I want right now is some matter of serenity, however ironic the notion.

Once I arrive in the client room, I find one medic on the floor beside Bliss's passed-out form, preparing to revive her with smelling salts.

"That won't be necessary," I interrupt him. "Force sent me to get her back to her room. You can test her there."

Without waiting for a response, I slide one arm under her knees and gingerly lift her into my arms, noting strangulation marks on her neck and bruises on her wrists and arms when I do. Somehow, Bliss remains unconscious, expression more composed than I've ever witnessed since my arrival. Why should I feel this much rage? Workplace abuse has always been common. Violence encouraged and demanded in every graphicker studio in the country. Even in the Aviary, I turned a blind eye to some of the assaults, especially when I was a new director. I only confronted them when they were a threat to *my* control.

But now…when I see the bruises like storm clouds marking her Pegasus-white skin, it takes more effort to control myself than ever. Sighing, I avoid staring down at her bare upper half, though the medic feels the need to remark on it once I arrive in the hall outside her door.

"The hidden daughter of the Temple. Curious, isn't it? They're twins. So similar. But he keeps this one behind the scenes without an exhibit but free for client interactions while the other is global-ly paraded but untouchable for anyone?"

"Force is a man of much puzzlement," I say, wheedling out of an explanation.

"She survives. Like other countless girls I've treated here," the medic goes on, though I don't care to listen.

Despite my outward indifference, my mind scoops up the last segment of information. The medic is an older gentleman, so I imagine he must have seen a few things during his time here. But for the first time, the knowledge sickens me. Despite knowing this girl—who is more woman—in my arms for only a brief time, I care more about the damage done to her now and in her past than I ever did for the girls in the Aviary. Nightingale, Blackbird, Pea-cock, even Mockingbird…it was simple to manipulate them into believing the lie. Serenity was the only difficult one.

For a moment, I consider Serenity in her sister's place. The possibility is one I can't stomach, so I disregard it. But every time I glance down at Bliss, I'm reminded of how physically similar they are. Day and night wearing the same faces, the same tender bodies.

Ridiculing myself once again for my wandering eyes, I trans-fer them to her suite door. Serafina waits beside it.

"I will take care of her now," she informs the medic.

"Of course, Serafina. Just send the blood sample down to me at your convenience."

He knows her name because she has drifted through the Pent-house like some sort of ghost. I suppose that's a half truth. The Penthouse itself still echoes reminders of Force's time with Serafi-na. Through Unicorn-themed sprite lites, however it bows to the Swan-themed art, the Penthouse holds half of Serafina's soul. Pro-vided my brother and I can form a solution to get all three women out of here, it will never hold Serenity's.

"If you can manage to set her down on her stomach, please," Serafina directs me.

At the same time I lower her body, I ensure the side of Bliss's face is pressed into the pillow. Serafina has healing cream already prepared as well as a serum. All for her appointment wounds.

"Hand me the cream," Serafina requests.

I'd rather leave the room, but I do as she asks out of respect, considering she did give birth to the girl I love…and her sister. My expectation is Bliss will wake when Serafina presses the cream to her wounds, but she remains still and serene in sleep. I assume the strangulation is what caused her to pass out. Hopefully, there will be no lasting repercussions, but I know that isn't true. She reminds me far too much of my unconscious Birds from the Aviary. Whatever the case, I intend to discuss her healing period with Force. Bliss needs more time. Or at least allow her some appointments with a CellGen. Ironically, Serenity's Immortal implant would be best suited for Bliss, but Force would never spend that much on his Yin.

"I've seen the way you look at my daughter."

So, that is why Serafina didn't ask me to leave. For the present, I indulge her.

"Serenity."

"Both of them."

"I beg your pardon." I intend it as a question, but it doesn't quite leave my mouth as one.

"Only two men have ever taken up residence in Serenity's heart. Unfortunately, one of them is gone. You keep trying to climb up on her pedestal, she will keep knocking you down."

At first, I give no response. Serafina is far too perceptive than I care to admit. Unlike Bliss, however, she doesn't try to manipulate or goad me. Unlike Serenity, she speaks reasonably, logically.

"Skylar is a good man. More than that, he is good for her. Don't you think it's time you stopped invading their love?"

She wipes up the last remnants of blood from Bliss's back. I continue standing beside the bed should she require anything else.

"With all due respect, Serafina, it's not in my nature to give up," I say to her.

"It takes a great amount of courage to let go of what you love, Luc. To admit you were wrong and move on."

"I'm not wrong," I deny, then glance at Bliss, expecting her to wake at any moment.

"Then, let me ask you two questions, and I will prove you wrong by them both."

"I'd rather you didn't."

"I am Serenity's mother." Serafina yanks my eyes to hers.

155

While I've always recognized the fire in Serenity's eyes coming from Force, her ice all stems from Serafina, who finishes, "So, with all due respect, Luc, you better damn well listen."

I keep my hands stiff at my side but remain where I am, giving her the benefit but displaying my lack of pleasure from the occurrence. Bliss still does not wake.

"I've learned a few things about you in the past few months from Skylar. You spent fifty million dollars for Serenity. You spent weeks in the Aviary and more weeks beyond its walls with her. You shielded her from the Temple. You killed for her on more than one occasion. You gave up your very Museum for her and followed her, prepared to do her bidding. You seduced her, which I will not address at this time. You have brought her to the very pinnacle of infamy through your costumes and fine exhibit renderings." She pauses, takes a deep breath, and finishes, "After all of this, Serenity still chooses Skylar. She will only ever see you as the man who exploited her. So, why do you refute it? More than refute it, you utterly deny it. Perhaps you hold tighter than even her father does."

I grit my teeth, clenching the muscles in my jaw. One more question until I can leave. My eyes drift to Bliss's statuesque features.

"And what is your second question?"

"If your feelings are so strong for my youngest, then why haven't you stopped looking at my oldest since you brought her into the room?"

Not answering Serafina, I turn around and depart. Silence, I suppose, is an answer in and of itself. At the moment, mine speaks volumes. Even when Serenity enters the room, I refuse to meet her eyes. Even if she's never managed to read my expressions as openly as I've managed to read hers, I'd rather not take the chance she read my guilt. Bliss's words from our first discussion gut me like ice shards; I'm a convicted felon according to their truth. Guilty of fantasizing Serenity's persona on Bliss's body. It would be so simple to indulge in it. To imagine it. Bliss could make it so simple. And I'm losing patience with Serenity's continuous rejection. Bliss would welcome me with open arms. The temptation bores into me. Whether I nurture it is my choice.

Force catches up to me in one of the halls. "I'm concerned about Serenity," he informs me.

In no mood to hear of his supposed concern for Serenity, I keep walking toward my room. Once I return to my sketches and am afforded the opportunity to study her anatomy again, I'm certain I will give up on this fruitless temptation. With the footage Force managed to acquire from Serenity's Skeleton Flower exhibits in the Garden, I can relive her moments again and again, foster my zeal, and capture every curve to render it for future display. My own method of having a piece of her even if I want all of her.

"She is withdrawn. Did you ever encounter her like this in the Aviary?"

His question diverts me from my train of thought, returns memories of Finch, of Raven, of Gull. Memories I don't wish to harbor.

"Yes." Perhaps if I keep my answers simple enough, he will relinquish the discussion.

"And what did you do to overcome it?"

No such luck.

I stop before my door, hand prepared on the knob. "What she needed most was empowerment and compassion. I took her to the Glass District. Let her select a child for me to purchase."

"For you to rescue..." he surmises.

"Yes."

"Thank you, Luc. Your information has been most helpful."

Thrilled beyond words, Force. I don't bother to say a word before I retreat into my suite, head straight for the bedroom, and turn on the sprite light on my canopy to select footage of Serenity. Removing my shirt and shoes, I discard them to the floor. Quite uncharacteristic of me, I leave them there.

Desire—sharper than ever—rouses a fire inside me when I see the outline of her form through the transparent shift of her Skeleton Flower costume. I swipe to a new image—her latest Swan exhibit and then to her Mermaid one.

I sit on the bed, then use my digital pen to sketch.

The moment I saw her, I knew I wanted her for the Aviary... but also for myself. I knew I would spend well beyond fifty million dollars to acquire her. And with her fulfilling my vision every time she enters one of those exhibits, I am closer than ever. Close to her but sensing her refusal. Knowing my brother's mouth is free to open hers, free to explore and taste and touch as much as he desires but knowing he will not drives me damn near mad.

Pausing after a few minutes, I examine the sketch I've just completed. Then, I curse.

It's not Serenity on the paper.

It's Bliss.

Twenty-five
SunShine

SERENITY

"WHERE ARE WE GOING?" I demand of my father, not the least bit enthusiastic about his dragging me away from my room.

Weekdays are my only reprieve from him. And times with my mother and Sky. This week, I also plan on trying harder with Bliss, but if my father decides to cart me all around the Temple, it's going to make it difficult.

He scans his barcode into the elevator, then punches a level for the halfway point of the Temple. As we descend, he waves a hand, triggering motion sensors that peel back the metal to reveal glass walls, allowing me to see a different side of the Temple. When I lean over to peer down at the vast sky-city, my father waves his hand again, slowing the motion. From here, I can see the camping level, which is a manmade forest wrapping around two floors. Strategically placed are cabins with artificial fire pits. Temple fantasies are boundless. If one is not provided, my father will carve out a new location by renovating an old level.

"Ahh…" Force gestures to a trail of hover boards gliding above our heads a couple of hundred yards away. "Looks like a tour is in progress."

"You really don't miss any money-making opportunities, do you?" I quip, planting my arms on the railing.

"You won't either when you take my place. I'm certain your resourcefulness will become just as limitless as mine. Particularly if you pair it with Director Aldaine's imagination," he hints, and I

159

respond with nothing more than an irked sigh.

"Where are we going?"

"I thought you might appreciate seeing your birthplace."

The Centre.

The elevator glides to a stop, and my father escorts me through the door and into a hallway connected to a skyway. From here, we're still a good distance from the ground, and all the city traffic and people look like dollhouse figurines and model car sets. Connected to the skyway is the infamous Centre—a vast skyrise itself with even more security than the Temple. Of course, we have security escorts.

"I thought you said you had a problem with security," I practically snort at my father when the automatic Centre doors open, revealing a detail of soldier-like men.

"I do, which is why I am in the process of screening candidates with the assistance of Director Aldaine. Perhaps you could recommend one? I seem to recall one young man who seemed to have much potential."

"He was just an Aviary security guard Luc employed at his retreat," I excuse, doing my best to remain nonchalant to protect Sky.

"Oh, come now, Serenity." Force rolls his eyes. "There should be no secrets between us."

I pause in the middle of the long white hall we've just entered where rows and rows of plaques adorn the walls, depicting various physicians and medical scientists in every field imaginable. Animated digital plaques that scroll to a sprite lite of the physician or scientist in action with more information. On my left are a series of windows to capture a view of the outside world—a city network of clogged arteries and veins. The Centre itself reminds me of a Tetris game with one high-rise and multiple lower ones branching out from its side—a domino effect. Other than private donations, countless grants, and tax dollars, I know the Centre's well-oiled machine also runs Temple money since so little funds go to the girls who work it. Those who choose the Centre are paid more, but they don't last as long—physically or psychologically.

"The Centre assists in every medical problem down to the smallest contraceptive," Force begins his monologue. "But our main purpose is dedicated to boosting fertility whether through research and development or new breeding methods or treatments for sexually transmitted diseases," he regales me with the Syndicate's side pet project—one they've had their hand in since its conception.

"And what about the new virus that's on the market now?" I challenge him, my eyes straying to the walls, whiter than cocoons. "Isn't that a problem for you since Neil's the only one with the vaccine?"

Laughing, Force just dips his head. "Ahh, I see he hasn't told you, has he? That naughty boy."

"What?" Impatient, I fold my arms across my chest, shifting my weight.

"He traded the vaccine. So, you're quite wrong it's only in his possession."

I drop my arms. "Why would he do that?"

"Because I offered him something he could not resist in return."

"Like what?" I tap my fingers against my arm, waiting.

Force opens his hand. "Access to you." He continues in spite of my surprise. "Of course I couldn't blame my own daughter, but after his assassination plot, do you think I would've allowed him to return to the Temple, much less see you again? During the weeks while you waited for your temporary prosthetics to wear off, his scientists finished the vaccine, and he agreed to trade it for an all-access pass to the Temple for himself and Aldaine."

Seems like I've underestimated my brother. I'll have to give him a tighter hug next time I see him.

Several medical staff members stop to address my father when we enter one birthing level. Doctors, nurses, receptionists—all pause to pay him some form of respect. Hearing a high-pitched shriek, I spin my head to the right, but the door is closed. The next one isn't, and I see a young woman in a hospital gown, abdomen swollen, as she walks around the room with a nurse standing nearby. I purse my lips and watch as the woman suddenly grips onto a wall railing, clenching her eyes in what I assume is mid-contraction.

Some of these girls have spent years upon years pregnant.

"We've discovered a way to speed up the rate so the nine-month gestation is unnecessary," Force says. "Test tube babies were considered for a time. Even invented an artificial womb that is still in use for lower birth rate months, but it's been proven life thrives much better in a real womb environment. Designer babies are for the elite. Ahh…here we are."

My father motions to a door. "I reserved the very best for Serafina."

The number doesn't matter to me. Only what's inside. I should have expected something like this—something that resembles a suite more than a hospital room. Two rooms rolled into one complete with couch and dining table, a three-hundred-and-sixty-degree view of the park, elaborate sculptures, and an opulent, state-of-the-art birthing bed. The walk-in bathroom features a large, circular whirlpool. I dredge up images from my mother's journal, but she had little to say about the room and much about me. It feels like entering a mausoleum—a ghost of my origin. Bliss should be here with me. We should share this together.

Force swings his hand as if it's a proud battle axe. "Would you care to see the nursery?" he offers.

I KNEW IT WAS A mistake to come here. The thought of all these babies growing up without mothers and fathers, pretty ones groomed for life in the Temple, others chosen for breeders, causes all the butterflies inside me to stumble like drunkards. I almost grin at the thought because I doubt I'd be particularly good at holding a baby. Looking down at my hands, I consider how fragile they seem but know they could hold lightning.

One nurse approaches the glass, arms coddling an infant she raises for us. A girl. Force nods his approval. The last thing I'd ever want is a girl—if I ever had one at all. Does Sky want children? I wonder why I've never bothered to ask him. Maybe it's because of Forget-Me-Not and Cosmos. Maybe I've even denied the notion all this time because I'm simply not interested in finding out. With so many deformed or frozen fetuses, stiller than abandoned birds' nests, I know I could never handle it.

"Ahh…punctual as usual." Force's tone lightens as he twists

his neck toward the entrance. "Good to see you, Queran."

At the mention of my preparer's name, I perk up, turning to see him progress into the nursery. Curious, I study the objects in his hand—small paper shapes dangling from two crisscrossed twigs: an infant mobile. That's when I notice the scores of other mobiles already hovering above the cradles. Mostly animals or stars and flowers, except for Queran's newest one. I press my fingers to the glass and smile as the nurse lowers the baby into the cradle, and Queran attaches the mobile with several swan shapes above her crib. Then, he straightens, looks at me from the side, and raises his hand.

"Queran, I will finish giving Serenity a tour. Once you're finished, you may accompany us back to the Temple."

Even as my father places a hand on the small of my back to lead me out, Queran holds up a finger, indicating he will join us. Only three mobiles for today, it seems. Just before we leave, I notice him scoop up a baby wrapped in a pink blanket, press his cheek to hers, and then hurry to join us.

Force mutters something that sounds like, "Probably an orphan thing".

I have no problem with Queran tagging along. He's dressed in what assume are his everyday clothes. Instead of the Penthouse-preparer uniform, Queran wears casual street clothes—nothing like my father's dramatic white suit with black vest accented by embroidered lace and digital-enhanced swans with a narrow gray scarf draped around his neck. No, Queran's style is more timid with his collar buttoned all the way to his neck along with a gray Newsboy hat and simple skinny jeans that seem to work for his figure.

Ahh…" my father croons, signaling to his temple. "I just received a Center alert. It seems we have a triplet birth. The first in the country this year. Would you care to accompany me?" He gestures toward the nursery door.

I shake my head. "No, I'd rather stay here."

A delivery should be a celebratory moment, but I won't be able to focus on the life without remembering the death of Forget-Me-Not's baby. And Cosmos. A shrill baby's cry off to my left startles me, but Queran wanders past me to scoop up the squealing infant. A nearby nurse smiles. I imagine they are understaffed and appreciate the volunteer help. While Queran hushes the infant, rocking him back and forth, I stare down at the sleeping babe right below me. So peaceful. Too peaceful for this place.

Out of the corner of my eye from beyond the glass window, I see a nurse wheeling a young girl down the hallway. My spine goes rigid. She looks like she's no more than fourteen. What I notice the most is the puckered flesh all along one side of her face, trailing down her neck, one side of her arm…old burn scars. What is she doing here?

Curious, I hasten out of the nursery, almost missing Queran staying close on my heels when I follow the nurse, who strolls the wheelchair into a nearby room. She doesn't notice me or Queran enter. Even if I could make demands to be here, my father would still be notified, so before the nurse can turn around, I grab Queran by the collar and yank him into the adjoining bathroom. Fortunately, he plays along.

"Shh…" I warn him, finger to my mouth even if it's too dark to see anything.

Queran doesn't respond but stays close. We wait. A curtain pulled, muffled words, a wall screen turned on…finally, footsteps recede and a door closes.

I'm about to open the door when I hear the girl call out, "Either you two peepers can give me a hand, or I can always press the nurse button."

When I step one foot out, the girl is in the process of moving the bed, metal legs screeching on the floor. It's only after she looks up at the ceiling that I realize she's trying to line it up with the vent.

Finally, the girl glances up and straightens, jaw dropping, but she picks it up rather quickly, though she shakes her head. "There's no way Lina's going to believe I met the Swan!"

Almost shell-shocked, I stand there, observing. Her soprano voice is not lilting in any way. Much too perky for that, as well as her movements. Nothing bird-like about them, she reminds me more of a cricket.

"Sunshine's the name?" she croons, frolicking up to me, extending a hand, gold-toned hair swinging around her shoulders.

After she's done shaking my hand, she prepares to do the same with Queran. Instead, he holds up a finger, retrieves a piece of paper, and folds it into a sun shape within a minute.

"What are you doing?" I point to the vent as he works.

Sunshine opens both hands as if it's obvious. "Escaping."

He presents her with the sun. Sunshine presses it to her chest. "Guy's got skills. Now, are you going to help or run to your daddy?"

I wish Sky were here.

"Where are you going to go when you get out?" I wonder even as I step onto the bed with her, prepared to lift her into the vent.

"Out where?" Sunshine places her hands on her hips, peers at me before a glimmer of recognition crosses her eyes. "Oh, not out there." She motions toward the window with its view of Temple transportation and the vast city beyond. "No, the Temple."

"Look, maybe you could just explain…" I suggest, glancing at Queran who nods in agreement.

Sunshine sighs, arms dropping. "Look, I tried to hide it as long as I could, but they found out, so it's my time to enter the breeding line. I'm not "Temple" quality if you catch my drift." She drifts two fingers to the scars all along the side of her body. "But Lina's in the Temple, and I want to see her before they inject me with that baby tracker."

"Lina?"

"She was the oldest in the Chick House," Sunshine explains. "They took her a few months ago to train her for Temple life."

I sigh, sweeping my gaze to the door. How long before my father returns? I'd wager not long; he probably only stays to watch the children emerge before leaving. He won't allow me to be alone for too much time. But after everything that's happened, I'd say he owes me more than a favor.

I turn my gaze to Sunshine. "Do you trust me?"

She blinks, gaze tossing to Queran, who winks at her.

"Answer me two questions first," she puts me to the test. "Was the shark real or just some sprite light?"

"His name is Sharky, and he's very real," I respond, ready to press for the next question. "What else?"

Sunshine assumes a challenging pose, arms crossed over her chest. Somehow, the hospital gown she wears makes her seem more imposing.

"What Bird would I be?"

I smirk. If I answer with anything cute or pretty, it would be a mistake. Sunshine's not that kind of girl. At first, I consider a Phoenix rising from the ashes because of her fire brands, but instead, I go with my gut.

"A buzzard. The kind with the leather faces and necks with all the wrinkles."

Sunshine's arms loosen from her chest at the same time she pronounces, "Oh, you're good." She gets down from the bed, and I follow but head for the door, promising to be back soon.

"I'll keep Paper Man company." Sunshine loops one arm around his, dragging him toward the bed. "Let's see what else you got."

Chuckling, I glance back at the two of them, knowing it would take all day for Queran to show Sunshine exactly what else he's got in origami terms. Right before I leave the room, I watch as he begins to fashion another shape and consider how she didn't ask if Queran was trustworthy. But no one would need to. Anyone would trust Queran with their life.

BLISS

WHEN I FIRST SEE ALL three of them enter the Penthouse together, my heart seizes in my chest. Was this Father's decision? No. All I need is one glimpse of Serenity's triumphant expression to know this was all her idea. But why? Doesn't she understand how the girl is just one more piece Force can use against her? He might wear his pride subtler, but I can see it in his cunning smirk every now and then. It was just as much a triumph for him, which makes me wonder if he has plans for the child already.

If he intends on turning her into a display, she wouldn't be in the Penthouse. Many girls are plucked from random Chick Houses and deposited for signature displays in the Temple. Men appreciate the young ones. Though the law prohibits client interactions for any under sixteen, *accidents* will happen—for a price.

She's just the type he'd look for with the halo gold hair, except for her ruined skin. The girl doesn't wear Serenity's defiance, but there is a measure of independence in her eyes. More than independence. When she raises her head, lifts it high even when Father addresses her, I recognize it as self-assurance. I excuse her body language as blissful youthful ignorance. Father will destroy that in no time if he has his wish—whatever that wish may be.

Despite my attempt to remain in the shadows, the girl is more aware than my sister because she's turned her head and points to me from down the hall.

"Another Swan!" She breaks into an eager trot.

I turn away, hearing Serenity call out after her.

"Wait!" I hear both their voices say at the same time. Directed on two different targets, of course.

The girl catches up to me, then takes me by the arm. As soon as I look at her, I avoid staring at her skin. Neither do I wince at the sight of her scars. I've born enough of my own. A different brand of fire for my flesh.

She looks me all up and down before remarking, "Lina would give her teeth to see this! She's the only one who's believed all those urban myths about the Swan twin."

"Is that what they call me?" I pass along the deriding comment.

Sunshine nods. "It is now."

It's no surprise. Even my urban myth must be shared with my little...I pause before considering the word.

Serenity reaches our sides, then cups the girl's shoulder. "Sunshine, this is my sister. Bliss." No, she doesn't hesitate to use the word.

"Sunshine," she chirps, her voice reminding me of honey and confetti. But there is something under that silver lining. A shameful cloud beyond.

She's not fierce like Serenity. Nothing about her reads discomfort. She might not be eager, but she's resigned. As if she understands the state of the world; she's aware of the demons drooling in the shadows.

"Serenity was just about to order brunch for us. Would you like to come?" Sunshine invites me.

I glance at my sister once. She just shrugs, which is an offering in and of itself.

I shake my head. "I'd rather not."

Sunshine doesn't press, but she does wave a hand. "Oh, I understand. The scars can be a bit daunting…"

In one move, she dethrones my resistance. Sighing, I shed my introversion off my shoulders for the present. I follow them.

Like the sun easing out from behind a cloud, Sunshine returns to her lively self. "Call it a gift."

At once, I roll my eyes. It's not often someone gets the drop on me. Certainly not a child. She managed to use her own skin against me.

Fortunately, Sunshine doesn't bother me with questions. She wants to know nothing about my background or why I've been hiding in the Penthouse all these years. On the contrary, she gives more than she takes from relating all the details she can about her life in the Chick House. Many names erupt from her mouth, and I lose track of them. Much of what she says is meaningful gibberish. Meaningful to her, gibberish to me.

"We bet on all things Temple-related. But we bet big on anything Swan-related or Faces of the Temple." She sways along beside Serenity. "I bet my dollhouse you'd be an unstoppable force ready to sweep the world! When your Mermaid display went international, I won Balloon's balloon set. But I gave it back the next day." She shrugs and joins her hands behind her back, fingers interlocking, their tips sharing secrets.

"Balloon?" Serenity questions.

"Her given name is Bluebird, but we call her Balloon."

"What was your plan once Airplane flew you all away?" Serenity asks after we're in her dining room sampling brunch. It's the first time I've been invited to eat with her. The dining area is far more beautiful than mine, which doesn't shock me. Every now and then, my eyes can't help but wander to the moving water sculptures, the liquid artwork rippling and dancing like ballerinas made of droplets. Serenity prefers the fish tank, much simpler in comparison.

My sister indulges in Sunshine's fantasy. A mistake if I've ever heard one. This child's fantasies will be crushed underfoot when the time comes. Better to let them go now while she can. They won't help her any. Mine never did.

"I found a treasure map at the dump one day." The dump is

really a landfill her caregiver takes her to because the Temple can't be bothered to invest in any proper toys for their orphanages. "Airplane would fly us, and I'd be the navigator. I'd help everyone find their way to the treasure." Sunshine tosses a grape in the air—a purple bubble falling until she catches it in her mouth.

I stiffen and cut into a grape, slicing it in half so it reminds me of Yin and Yang. "And what treasure would that be?"

"Well, it's not really a treasure. It's a castle." Sunshine's hands spread, fan-like. "A gigantic castle with a moat full of dolphins with razor teeth. As soon as you step foot on that land, you grow bat wings. The only way to get into the castle is to fly in."

My sister smiles, intently listening to everything.

"What's inside the castle?" she wonders.

Sunshine waves a hand. "Our families, silly. Oh, and Falcon made sure to include her imaginary boyfriend one day. Guess he looks a lot like that sexy Aviary director."

It's the first time I've noticed Serenity wince at the mention of Luc. She's spent all this time refusing to cave in to his advances, and it makes me wonder if she'll ever falter. Or perhaps *he* will first.

"Any imaginary boyfriends for you?" Serenity diverts the subject.

"Me? Not a chance." The girl doesn't make a face. She just dismisses the notion as if it's no more than an irritating static electricity. "I wouldn't have time for a boyfriend. I'd be too busy transforming into my other form to protect the castle."

Serenity taps a finger to her chin. "Let me guess—a dragon?"

"Close. Tyrannosaurus Rex." Sunshine winks and chomps down on her fifth slice of bacon. "But you can be the dragon if you want to, Serenity."

"I'm allowed to come?"

"Of course."

"What about Bliss?" She motions to me.

Sunshine licks the grease off her fingers. Eyes me. I meet her gaze head-on. "She can come. We need a good ghost haunting the place to make it authentic. But I think she'd only transform if she really had to."

"Why?" Serenity swings her head toward me and back to Sunshine. "What do you think she'd be?"

Sunshine ponders while raising a strawberry to her mouth. "Phoenix. Hands down, a phoenix. Bliss is a survivor. She'll always rise from the ashes."

I excuse myself, then get up from the table.

"Bliss, wait—"

"Let go of my arm, Serenity," I request through gritted teeth. "Just leave me alone."

This is her trying again when she hugs me, careful to string her arms around my untarnished neck and not scar-riddled back. I'm not interested in her consolation right now. That's all Serenity wants to do…console. Treat me like some helpless victim. She'll never see me as anything but broken.

At least Sunshine doesn't apologize. No, she's rather smug, sitting there. Serenity is much easier to handle than this perceptive little skin sack. Even her scars taunt me. She reminds me of a future I once imagined when I was still a child. I can't afford childish fantasies. Nothing ever changes.

Sunshine knows. Serenity doesn't. And the child is having a ball with her.

I ignore Luc as I pass him in the hallway.

"Is she in her room?" he pauses to ask.

"She has a visitor. Not male." I'll have to be careful, considering I wrapped the last two words in a layer of loathing.

"Bliss."

It's the first time he's touched me. Just a brush of his fingers on my arm.

"Everyone has a price, Luc," I remind him. "Mine is simply cheaper than Serenity's."

"You don't have to do this."

I recognize his pursuit when he steps into my circle. Not as extreme as my sister, I only retreat halfway but still offer him a dangling Swan feather to whet his appetite.

"If your bed ever gets too lonely, Luc, you know where to find mine."

Twenty-six

SuITor

SERENITY

"WHAT WAS THAT?" SUNSHINE REFERS to the dull thud coming from upstairs.

A radar goes off in my head because Force interrupted my breakfast and dragged me away on the tour before I had the chance to talk to Sky. Much less feed him.

My eyes flick to the staircase, and Sunshine is up faster than blown glitter. The next thing I know, I'm chasing her up the stairs and into my bedroom where she nearly collides with Sky.

"Excuse me!" I hear her exclaim just as I hurry through the doorway. She turns to me as soon as I arrive. "You realize there's some sort of demigod in your bedroom, right?"

Sky folds his arms across his chest, muscles bulging as he smiles down at her. "Demigod, I like that."

"Got any other sexy beasts in here?" Sunshine asks before wandering around, even going so far as to peer under the bed.

Pleased she's taking everything in stride, I drop my arms to my sides and confess, "Sorry, no. Sky's the only one."

"Friend of yours?" She jerks a thumb toward him.

I shrug, dropping my hands to my sides. "More like a secret friend."

"How secret?" she wonders, summoning the sprite light program on the table next to my bed.

"*Very* secret," Sky echoes, tilting his weight toward her.

Sunshine makes a shushing motion with her fingers. "I'll just say he's your invisible friend. This is really cool." Her finger lights on the screen, shifting the bed canopy and walls around us into different environments. She taps into another app. A moment later, the walls around us revolve into framed water. My father's latest addition along with the shifting water sculptures he installed. A way of making me feel comfortable. My room has turned into an underwater scene.

"No way!" gushes Sunshine, spinning around and flitting toward one of the water walls.

Upon hearing the knock at the door below, I groan and head for the railing to shout, "What?"

"Serenity," I hear the muffled voice from behind the door. "It's Luc."

"Go away!"

To Luc, my commands are more invitations because he opens the door. Sunshine appears from behind me to peek at him.

"The Aviary director?" she nearly squeals. "You're just a sexy man magnet, aren't you?"

She scrambles down the stairs but stops herself short from leaping on Luc. Instead, she stands right in front of him, eyes digesting his face, hands wringing together. "Look, if I don't get a picture with you for Lina, she'll tar and feather me!"

"Well, we can't have that now, can we?" Luc replies while tapping his barcode for his arm interface for a candid Penthouse screenshot. I roll my eyes as he coils an arm around her shoulder, and Sunshine poses with a Shaka 'hang-loose' hand sign. I can't believe that ancient gesture is trending again.

"I'll take a photo with you, too!"

At the sound of the third voice invading my suite. I groan even more, but at least this one is a little more welcome than the last. And I did promise to give him a tighter hug.

Sunshine's eyes go wide. "No way! Nile Bodelo! I recognize you from like every magazine ever." She shakes out her gold hair in disbelief.

"Why, thank you." He offers her a petite bow, hand framing his chest. "Name's really Neil. But don't tell anyone."

"It'll be our little secret." Sunshine is stockpiling secret after secret, knitting them tight into the spaces between her clenched hands as she takes a picture with Luc and then Neil.

"Say MagiTouch," my brother croons, referring to the startup tech company that revolutionized lasers years ago so people could touch them and now interact with them every day.

"So formal," Sunshine mocks. "All the kids just say "magic" nowadays."

Neil corrects himself and zooms in, pressing the side of his face against hers, careless of her scarred flesh.

"What do you want, Neil?" I ask from the balcony.

"So hostile," he emphasizes. "Is your boy toy around? He and I need to have a little chat."

"Sky's in the bedroom." I wind my head around to add, "He *should* be in the rafters."

Sky just shrugs, peeking his head around the corner. "You didn't bring me breakfast. Was just seeing if there was any food."

Sunshine shakes her head, laughter sprinkling the air like comet dust. "Men. If they're not thinking with their stomachs, they're thinking with their—"

"And what are *you* doing here?" I ask Luc.

"I, too, need to have a few words with my brother."

"Then, come up," Sky dares, nudging my side with hands held up, goading palms out. "I'm right here."

Sunshine perks up at the information. "Two sexy beasts are brothers?" She darts a finger back and forth between the two of them. "Ahh…" Her eyes narrow. "I can see it."

"I'm in no mood for a confrontation," Luc adds while keeping his arms at his sides.

"That's cause you're a lily-livered coward," Sky answers.

Sunshine eyes the two of them before she makes another connection, though her voice is a little softer this time when she says, "Um…eesh—history. Should I go?"

I groan a little, tilting my head toward the men. "Maybe we both should," I offer just before making for the stairs.

Before I get the chance, Sky reaches for my hand. He doesn't tug or drag me back like Luc would, but he squeezes the skin there for an invitation. I welcome the brush of his mouth on mine, bearing no more than the weight of a swan's wing. Not demanding. Not an exhibition for Luc. Just a parting reminder for our sake alone. I kiss his cheek, and Sunshine whistles low, but Neil prefers a high-pitched one. In return, I give him an obliging nudge from my elbow followed by that tight hug.

"Come on, Sunshine. Come on, Neil."

"But, sis! I wanted to watch," he protests just before I grab him by the ear. "Ow! Ow! I'm coming."

He trots out like the little lapdog he is, but his title is not lost on Sunshine, who remarks, "Sis? You two?" She points to us as I close the door. "Ahh...I can see it," she repeats her earlier statement. "Seriously, you should hand out a family tree diagram."

"What did you want to discuss with Sky?" I ask my brother.

Neil stuffs his hand in his pockets, glancing to the door. "Was thinking there might be a way for me to bring him in. Daddy's upping security lately, looking for new guards. If Sky can reach out to his connections, I can do the same. Next month, Force is having a try-out. Happens twice a year. Security guards and potential ones compete in an arena—giant obstacle course with a boxing match at the end—to see who's the most capable. The winner gets Penthouse duty. Was thinking we could get boy toy a prosthetic like we did for you."

I sigh. "Only one obvious problem. Boxing match? I'd say punching is one thing you'd want to avoid with prosthetics."

Neil curses, nostrils flaring like they're puffing out a storm. "Didn't think of that. Could go permanent," he suggests.

I narrow my brows so low I imagine they become velvet curtains drowning out the light. "Never!"

"Whoa, no offense, Serenity." Neil holds up his hands. "I'm sure he'd do it for you."

"I'm sure he would. But I like Sky's face just the way it is." I lean up against the door.

"How did you meet him?" Sunshine interjects, referring to Sky.

"On the day I was born."

"Oh, *long* history, then?"

"Very."

"I was wondering why you guys were so intense." She whips her head back and forth between Neil and me, scanner eyes wandering up and down. "Guess you're all pretty intense."

Shrugging, Neil takes out an electronic cigarette. "Blood can do that."

"Blood always does that."

I almost flinch at the sound of my father's voice. If he wasn't approaching from the other end of the hall, I'd be concerned he'd heard more than the last bits of our conversation.

"Having a little party, Serenity?" He sways toward me, posture playful, exaggerative hand on his chest. "I'm hurt. You should have invited me."

"Spontaneity doesn't afford much opportunity for invitations," I quip, glaring at him.

"Well," Neil inhales the word before cupping my shoulder and leaning over to kiss my cheek, "I'm off for a photo shoot in Madrid. Be back next week for your exhibit, sis. Ta!"

Chicken.

After Neil departs, my father turns to inform me, "We'll be having a guest for dinner."

I roll my eyes. "Like we do every night."

"You may bring Sunshine if you wish." His fingers flutter toward her like a bouncing swing. "Aldaine?" Force turns at the door opening behind us. "Have a fondness for standing in the middle of an empty suite?"

For a moment, Luc stares at me, and I poison my features as much as possible, imagine a hot-blooded horse with lightning in her wake charging from my eyes into his.

Luc squares his shoulders. "She slammed the door in my face. I was collecting my thoughts before I followed her."

"Persistence is a trait I admire, my fine young man." My father touches Luc's shoulder, more affection in that gesture than I like. It's obvious he still has hopes for me to choose the former director.

I grimace, eyeing them. "Goes both ways."

"Yes," Force sighs. "I'm afraid you two are equally matched in that department. Your horns will always lock together."

I set a hand on Sunshine's back. "I'm taking her to see my shark."

"Provided a new security member escorts you," Force hastens to order.

I want to tell him I'm not an idiot, but I don't bother.

"WHERE'S SUNSHINE?" SKY ASKS ONCE I've returned to the bedroom later, fully prepared in my ensemble for dinner. Considering how Sky's eyes dance across my form, I know I've chosen right.

"With Queran. I'm meeting her soon, but I promised her I'd talk to you first. We're going to get her out."

Sky nods, lips pressing together, already considering the complexities. "I can make a call for pickup tonight."

"But she needs to go down to Temple first."

"Run that by me again."

Exhaling, I onto the bed. "I promised her she could trust me. Her best friend, raised with her, went to the Temple first. Training level or something. Sunshine wants to see her first."

Sky rubs his chin as he starts pacing. If I could peek into his head, I would see a dozen different centipede thoughts crawling around a Temple-sized maze of countless floors. Dead end here. Tripwire there.

"It's riskier," Sky finally concludes, pausing mid-step. "Training levels have more security measures."

"I made a promise, Sky." My voice falls along with my eyes as I consider the notion of Sky getting caught. What my father would do to him. Or worse…use Sky against me, get me to give something up.

Then, I feel the bed shift. Sinking a deep indent into the mattress, Sky cups the side of my face, urging it toward him. His eyes travel across mine, slow and steady.

"Your promises are my promises. I'll do what I can."

This time, I kiss him. And not just a brush of my lips.

"PAPER MAN'S A MAKEUP GOD!" Sunshine exclaims once I enter the studio, which is more like a souped-up makeup room. Up to this point, mine and Bliss's preparations have simply taken place in her attached sitting room, but this studio is another option.

At first, I'd bucked against this *preparation* notion. If Sunshine wanted to dress up for dinner, she could have used the BODY, but she was curious.

"I want to know what it feels like before you go into an exhibit," she'd spoken. I cringed, not wanting someone as young as her drawn to such a thing. If it weren't for Queran, I wouldn't have folded as easily as a feather.

I study Queran as he braids the final strand into a conglomerate of intricate designs on her head before admitting, "Yes. The preparations are difficult. The results are not."

"I imagine it must take a lot of courage to be vulnerable like that. To let someone else touch your skin." She nods to my preparer, smiling, bits of golden rays on her lips.

I bite the inside of my cheek. "I think respect is required even more." I sound like my sister, so I add one of my own statements. "Courage is necessary when you don't want someone to touch your skin. Courage and fortitude."

"And strength," she adds, squaring her shoulders. "Something we don't have as much as our male counterparts."

"Willpower can trump strength."

"Damn right."

I don't give her false hope. If Sky's plan fails, she will need survival. Survival and a thousand triggered coping mechanisms. Even life as a breeder will come with coping mechanisms.

At first, I straighten but then glance at Sunshine as she lowers her head, her lashes a shroud over her eyes, hands placated in her lap as Queran applies her makeup.

"I can imagine *you'll* be the one everyone looks at tonight!" She changes the subject. "Just look at your hair and your bling."

Queran pauses as Sunshine gawks at the high-tech gold filigree latched onto my arm. Miniature sunbeams fan out from its edges. The choker I wear is pure gold with a digital pendant of swirling mood glitter. Tonight, the glitter is feisty. Apart from the feathers raining down my back, the dress itself could be a gold chandelier.

Queran isn't offended when Sunshine stands to marvel. Even if I did use the BODY tonight, he still knows his hands are sacred.

"You almost look like some fire swan," Sunshine remarks, finger trailing along one of my gold feathers. "No one will be looking at me tonight."

I'm counting on that.

"Sunshine..." I approach her and cup her shoulder. "You're

not coming to dinner."

Sunshine winces, twisting her shoulder out of my hand. Immediately, I realize my mistake at touching the scarred side of her body. I should have known better.

"I'm keeping my promise," I alert her, hoping my words will make up for that faux pas.

Her eyes lift. "You can get me to Lina?"

"Yes. And out of the Temple."

Sunshine's mouth falls open. The first time it does with nothing coming out.

Despite how I've kept my voice low, Queran straightens nearby, revealing he overheard every word. I just hope my willingness to share this in front of him doesn't betray me.

"Thank you," Sunshine finally utters after a few seconds.

That's all I need. Placing a hand on her back, I guide her toward the door and whisper low, "Wait for me by the elevator." I'll get her as close to the training level as I can. Sharky is the best excuse. Sky knows to meet us there.

Fortunately, Sunshine doesn't ask any other questions, but she does turn around, scampering to Queran for a moment. I think he is just as surprised by her embrace as I am.

Retrieving his origami present from earlier, Sunshine wags it in the air and proclaims, "I'll keep it forever. They couldn't burn the sun out of us." She stands on her tiptoes and kisses his cheek, urging a smile. "Stay true, Paper Man."

That's when I realize why Sunshine felt a pull to Queran. Two sides of the same coin. Except his scars are internal. And chemical. Hers are external. And physical. They know each other in a way I never will. Just like me and Bliss.

And for the first time, I think it might be okay...to not understand.

But I still need to tell her...

"WHAT DO YOU WANT, SERENITY?" Bliss opens her door. Between the silk robe sticking to her skin and her unkempt hair, I know she's just finished with a client. Sunshine will probably have made it to my room by now. We don't have long.

"I thought you might want to say goodbye." I rush through my words. "Sky's getting her out tonight."

At first, Bliss lifts her brows, eyes opening a little to betray her surprise, but her defenses only shift in the moment before she adopts her usual indifferent posture.

"Why would I want to do that?"

"Bliss." I touch her arm, just a trickle of my fingertips across the skin there. "Sometimes, hope is for real. It's real tonight."

"And you think nothing of the repercussions of your actions?"

I shake my head. "Not tonight. All that matters is Sunshine. I won't let the Temple squash it."

Bliss huffs, hands storming her hips. It's the first time I've seen this much emotion from her. "You realize what she's been doing this whole time?"

I shrug, fingers start fiddling with one another. "She's been having a ball."

"At your expense."

"So?"

Bliss sighs, arms dropping to her sides. "So, you do have some measure of self-deprecation."

I shift my weight. "She's just a kid."

"Hope is a dangerous thing. What happens if you fail?"

"*We* won't fail."

Bliss shakes her head but glances back at her bedroom as if debating on whether to join me. I can already see the surrender in her eyes.

Finally, "Give me a couple of minutes to get dressed."

Twenty-seven

PaRaSol

SKY

WHEN SHE REPEATED THE WORD "promise," I recognized that glint in her eyes. She was adamant. Relentless. My unstoppable force.

Given how long it will take me to reach Sharky's level, I don't waste any time. I just follow the virtual map in my head until the rafters lead me to the elevator shaft. Free-climbing is the quickest way to get there unless I can hitch a ride on the elevator, but it's anchored fathoms below. No time to wait. I chalk it up to my work out for the day. Not the first time doing this. Going up can be easier than getting down sometimes. If I had all the time in the world, I'd crawl through all the vent shafts that crisscross their way through each level, but expedience is necessary.

If anyone can get Sunshine out, that 'ol bird can.

About a quarter of the way down, my legs start to shake. I pause in the middle of the shaft to wipe a sheen of sweat off my head. At least the chalk I stole from the supply closet is proving its usefulness. Keeping my legs steady in the shaft footholds, I coat more of my hands in it and keep going. This is anything but mindless. At all times, I keep myself sharp. Least the training level is only a few floors down from Serenity's shark.

I edge my way into level 990 rafters, then make my way to the auditorium where I find Sunshine standing next to the tank. No Serenity yet. She'll be here soon.

"Nice fish, huh?" she comments as I trudge down the stairs, my hands stuffed deep into my pockets to conceal the shaking. By

180

tomorrow, I'll have a well-earned badge of blisters.

"Don't let Serenity hear you calling him that."

She points a finger to the tank. "He won't come this way."

I shake my head. "Nope, something he only does when she's around. Got a special bond with her." But I'd still prefer if it wasn't tested frequently. If anything good can be said of Force, at least he's planning to keep her busy with plenty more exhibits before he rotates her previous ones.

Sunshine shivers. "I'd be scared stiff to get in the water period."

"No good at swimming?" I prop one arm up against the tank.

"Not really. Now, the idea of hang-gliding sounds pretty fun."

"Really? Not base-jumping? I'd be all over that." I kid around with her. She reminds me of Serenity when she was younger but just a little. Serenity's always been more intense. Sunshine's still reserved, but I guess she's got her own sort of magic. That's what Serenity's drawn to—the ones who have magic. She's also got some sharp edges to her but on the inside. Not on the outside.

"Neither of you are thinking big enough," my girl's voice cuts through our pithy examples. "Skydiving would be the ultimate thrill."

I nod to the figure behind her. "What about you, Bliss?"

I have no qualms about acknowledging her. No fear of exposure. If Serenity has brought her here, it means she trusts Bliss enough to let her in on our secret. In either case, there's no going back.

Serenity's sister maintains her typical stoic pose as she responds, "I prefer to keep my feet on solid ground."

"If the Temple can be defined as solid ground," I quip.

"It's solid enough for me." Her arms remain at her sides, stiffer than totem poles. Her eyes are waging a war within her body. I can tell by the way she keeps glancing to Sunshine.

"Fair enough."

Bliss raises her chin. "I'm more interested in knowing who you are."

"Would you like to make the intro, Ser? If you can tear yourself away from sushi there."

"Shh, Sharky." She smoothes her fingers along the glass, cooing to her new pet as he predictably rolls his body close to the tank's front. "He didn't mean anything by it."

Sunshine takes advantage of the opportunity to get a closer look at Sharky, and she and Serenity banter a little back and forth. Guess it's up to me, then.

"Skylar Lace." I extend a hand. "Friends call me Sky."

Bliss is more observant than I previously assumed. She pauses to eye my sore palms, the redness under a layer of chalk, and the way my fingers falter—a leftover from my time in the shaft.

"Skylar Lace." She murmurs the last name, identifying with it immediately—the same as Serenity's—before turning to her sister. "Serenity, is there something you want to share?"

Serenity sighs, heaving her shoulders. "It's a long story."

"You *will* tell it later," Bliss states, voice firmer than a stone fist.

"Time for goodbyes first." I can tell the effort it took Serenity to say that. The time has come for Sunshine to go.

"You know I was prepared," Sunshine informs her, shrugging.

"Now, you can prepare for something else," Serenity replies, eyes fervent as lightning striking steel.

"Don't look a gift horse in the mouth," I echo.

Sunshine waves her hand. "I was never trying to get your sympathy."

"No." Serenity shakes her head. "No, just my trust."

The child twirls her finger around. "No, that's turned around. I was supposed to trust you. The whole *buzzard* thing…"

Serenity interjects, standing firm, denying, "I'm trusting you more."

When her gaze flicks to me, to Bliss, I watch Sunshine as she picks up on it. And chuckles. "Right. Cause the Yin twin isn't the only one with secrets. This whole thing would make one great show. So, why trust me so much?"

My girl beams. "Because you liked Serenity more than the Swan."

Sunshine opens her arms, leaning in to hug Serenity. The significance of how she presses her scarred cheek to Serenity's flawless one is not lost on me. But I'm not focused on them so much as Bliss. It's the first time I've seen her waver a little. First time I've seen those skyscraper eyes soften. Not melt but soften. First time her posture's has sunk. She purses her lips, but it seems to take more effort. Like folding over thick leather instead of skin.

"Live for them, girl," I interrupt the tender moment, leveling with Sunshine. "Best advice I can give. Make mistakes, have fun, grow up, do some good. I'll shut up now."

"Your muscles are better at talking." Sunshine winks, then gives me a light punch on the arm, but it feels more like a tap... from a lamb's head. "I guess this is what flying away feels like."

"Or floating," Serenity suggests instead.

"A floating parasol."

All three of us turn to look at Bliss. She joins her hands in front of her and explains, "That's what you remind me of—a floating parasol sailing in the wind."

Sunshine beams as bright as her name. "A parasol. Parasols soak up the sun but protect others from it. I guess that's my other name."

Judging by Sunshine's personality, she's the type who will work well in the Sanctuary. Even as Parasol. I wish I could make promises. If I could, I'd tear down the walls of that Chick House and get all those kids to the Sanctuary where they belong. I can't dwell on them. Drive myself crazy with the endless circle of thoughts like a dog chasing its tail; simple metaphors work for me. Saving one or two girls like this might not make up for all the others who are stuck, but just helping one to slip through the cracks can make all the difference in the world. Makes me feel more like a man than I've ever felt free-climbing an elevator shaft, throwing a punch, or taking a beating.

I never miss an opportunity to kiss Serenity goodbye. Never know if it might be my last time. This time, I kiss her harder. One moment to taste her before pulling away to escort Sunshine up the auditorium staircase toward the vent shaft opening.

I might be built like Hercules, but even I have my limits. Won't be going down that shaft again, especially not with a fourteen-year-old girl attached to my back. Slow and steady through each vent shaft level wins the race. Since it's night, the exhibits will be packed, which gives us one plus and one minus. Plus: busy time means enough noise to cover up the sound of our movements. Minus: Lina might not be alone.

"Going down, Sunshine," I instruct her just before lowering her at a vertical angle.

For her first time, she sure is fearless. Bet she'd squeal going down the slide if I didn't warn her not to say anything. Once I join her on the lower level, we peek through the cracks to see a crowd of men below our heads taking in the sights of the Arabia Level.

Sunshine kisses my cheek. "It's Parasol."

"Not until I get you out of here," I remind her. "One mission at a time."

"Aww, you didn't even blush."

"You're welcome," I keep my voice low and motion her forward.

The vent shaft on this level doesn't connect to the training room, but it does to the room next door. Unfortunately, it's a client interaction room—in use. The moans immediately flood the shaft, and I smack my hands over Sunshine's ears.

"I'm fourteen, Sky. Not five," she whispers, eyebrows lifted.

Be that as it may, it doesn't mean she needs to hear it.

"You'll thank me later." Even if she can't hear the words, she's read my lips, judging by the roll of her eyes.

"*Now* you're blushing," she points out but fortunately doesn't giggle.

Another moan followed by a high-pitched shriek.

Except this time, Sunshine rips my hands from her ears and leans in closer, eyes narrowing to see through the vent gaps. I keep my eyes on her, not who she's looking at. Sunshine lets her guard down. Eyes steeped in recognition…and pain. I should've predicted this could've happened. Age requirements be damned. This shit has been going on for generations. Security doesn't care. Chaperones don't care. Managers don't care. Everything's available for a price.

Even after the bed stops shaking, Sunshine doesn't. Her hands continue to tremble because we both can hear her friend's whimpers. The whimpers she can only make now the damn sex buyer is out of the room. A series of gasps follow. A sudden squeal. And finally, a sigh loud enough to swallow the room before I hear footsteps, a door opening, and the shower starting.

Sunshine nods to me, so I open the vent shaft and lower her

into the room. A few minutes later, her friend Lina opens the door to the bathroom, a wisp of steam puffing around her robed body.

"Sunshine!" Lina startles, eyes drifting back and forth between the two of us, tugging her robe closer to her skin.

Even under the circumstances, Sunshine doesn't wait to grab her friend and pull her in close. Sunshine's scars soak up Lina's tears as she asks her again and again, "What happened?

And I have a feeling we're going to be here longer than I thought.

SHE KEEPS HER DISTANCE FROM me. That's fair. Sunshine directs her to the couch in the corner of the room.

"The first day, it wasn't bad at all," Lina begins to explain. "They gave me a room, new clothes, showed me how to use the NAILS and the BODY. I was the youngest but not the only trainee. The second day, the chaperones took us to the training studios and taught us to dance. They said I was learning well. Then, things changed…"

Shadows etch into her voice, and I cross my arms over my chest, mouth grim because I can see where this is going.

"They said they needed to teach me how to dance right. How to move my body in a different way. I knew it was expected. And they said it was empowering. Just like all the mags across the country. So, I learned to dance that way. And when the BODY was programmed with lingerie outfits, I knew it was all part of the training.

"But the next time I went to the studios, there was an audience. And the first time…it happened, the older girls…" Lina arches her neck, straining to get the words out, "they told me, 'Well, what did you expect?'." She gestures to the room.

"Do you want to go with Sunshine?" I don't hesitate to ask her. Damned if I'm taking an extra risk.

Lina meets my eyes for the first time, but they almost cause mine to tip. Too ashamed of my own fucked up Y chromosome that makes up almost half the population.

Sunshine speaks for me. "Sky's a…friend. He can get us to the Sanctuary."

Lina balks at her. "That's why you're here. You're gonna get us killed, Sunny! You're gonna ruin everything."

"It's already ruined," Sunshine points out. "I saw what happened, Lina. You don't want to be here. They lied to you. They don't care if the law is broken."

"And how do you know we can trust him?" Lina jerks a finger toward me, and I don't try to defend myself. I have no grounds.

"Because the Swan does."

Lina pauses, studies me, eyes jerking back to her friend. "You met the Swan?"

"It's a long story. If you come with me, I'll tell you all about it."

Twenty-eight
RePerCussions

SERENITY

"WHERE IS SHE?" FORCE CONFRONTS me in my room. I don't move from my place on the balcony, imagining the gold in my dress fusing to the marble floor. I'm immovable.

"Who?"

"Don't play coy with me," my father warns as he progresses up the stairs. "I've searched the Penthouse floors. I've checked surveillance. You accompanied the child to your shark tank. After which, she vanished."

"People disappear in the Temple all the time," I goad him with well-timed irony.

"And the disappearance of a fertile girl does not reflect well on the Temple. Or the Centre." He reaches the last step, brows positioned low.

I hoist my chin high. "You couldn't care less about her. You're only sore because I one-upped you this one time." Turning to face him, I lodge a verbal cannonball at my father. "Because for once, something didn't go according to your precious plan." I rake my nails into the balcony behind me.

Force advances toward me until his shadow eclipses me like black frost. "Was it Luc?"

I keep my mouth shut.

"I'm not going to ask again."

I give him nothing.

"Very well." My father drops his arms to his sides. "You want to play this game? You forget I've been playing it much longer, Serenity. And someone else accompanied you to the tank room."

Bliss.

The lower door of my bedroom opens to reveal my sister.

"Good girl, Mara," Force commends as she enters the room. "You always come when you are called."

Panicked, I zero in on Bliss, almost regretting inviting her to say goodbye to Sunshine...until I realize she isn't speaking. Then, I comprehend what's going on. My father doesn't want the truth from Bliss; he still wants it from me.

In Force's hands is a whip.

No.

He turns his back, which is a mistake. My mistake is assuming he's unfamiliar with my patterns because he sidesteps me when I charge. Air can't hold my weight, and I tumble down the stairs, knocking my head into one of the railings.

Each fall is unique. Like a snowflake. I never get used to them. All the lights around me blur, and every movement is unbalanced. The opposite of yin and yang. It's just all Yang teetering on the world's axis. Someone's taken a battering ram to my temple. Reaching up, I feel blood. Pain infects me. For the first time, I double over, whimpering, coughing—so close to vomiting. The floor pirouettes, the walls join its dance, and I can't get up without risking falling more.

It turns out I don't have to because Force scoops me up from the floor.

"Now look what you've gone and done."

Out of the corner of my eye, I notice Bliss following us. It's the first time I read concern in her eyes.

Force doesn't brush the hair from my eyes when he lifts me into his arms and heads for my bedroom. All he does is rub his thumb across the wound on my forehead, causing me to flinch from the pain and whimper again. My vision still refuses to clear. My throat feels full of acid. I croak out the only word I can define with my father. "No."

"Hush now," he orders as he puts me down on my bed. "You've brought this on yourself. We bring out the best in each other; we bring out the worst, too."

Even lying down, I'm riding on some warped merry-go-round. My father's figure stretches, languid. Something thuds in my ear repeatedly. Nausea envelopes me. He wanted this to happen. To teach me a lesson. This is my punishment.

My father orders a medic and splicer since the floor practically bludgeoned my head. All my butterflies are dropping, wings fluttering in and out. Too weak to fly. He stands to speak to the arriving medic, and I double over, coughing again, feeling bile rising in my throat. A minute later, a searing pain engulfs my temple just near the wound, but Force keeps me at bay with his hands holding my shoulders down.

"You'll be numb soon," he coos in my ear.

His voice is too muffled.

All my butterflies rear up, lightning smacking their wings back and forth as my father brings the splicer to my forehead and starts stitching up the wound himself. Bruises forming on other parts of my body overshadow the dimming pain of my head. My mind still feels puffy—thoughts more like swirling cotton balls. But each one is heavier than a paperweight.

Then, I feel a sharp twinge in my arm.

A sedative.

"We have a few minutes left," Force declares and stands, directing Bliss to the middle of the floor. Up until now, I haven't realized she was standing on the other side of the bed, her eyes pinpointed on me. Just after Force's command, she purses her lips. She's hesitating. Because of me.

My fall wouldn't deter my father. No, it only strengthens his resolve. Do this now while I'm too weak to fight back. If I tell the truth, he'll hurt Sky. If I say nothing, he'll hurt Bliss. Worse than ever before.

Bliss kneels.

Force walks toward her.

"No," I moan. I clench my eyes, try to move, but my body feels heavier than my shark. I'm running out of words, too.

It's too difficult to fight. Lightning can't counteract the sedative.

"Tell me the truth," Force turns, urging me one last time.

I squeeze my eyes shut, feeling one tear battle its way down my cheek.

Force raises his whip.

I open my eyes. And there is Sky with one hand clenched around my father's, warring with him for the whip. And winning. Like the half-cocked devil he is, Force tilts his head to observe Sky just before ordering all his Penthouse security. At once, Sky shoves him back, assuming control of the whip. Sweet adrenaline bursts inside me, giving me just a minute or two at most. Enough to see Sky is tempted to use the weapon, but I already know he won't. Because he's not me.

Sky chucks it instead, glances once at Bliss, and then makes a beeline straight toward me. Somehow, I muster up the energy to crawl onto my hands and knees, but I don't make it out of the bed.

Security has arrived. All I can do is watch.

Bliss watches, too. She hasn't moved once from her knees.

I hear a thud as Sky body slams a guard to the floor. Five more wrestle him to the ground. There is my father studying him, recognition in his eyes; he remembers Sky from the retreat.

Sky takes out another security guard until two more arrive. Seven against one. Finally, they stun him, but thanks to the Garden, he's built up an immunity to electric shock. They must pin him to the floor, muscles holding down every inch of him. Only after they manage to accomplish this feat does my father approach.

"Force—"

"Quiet, Serenity," my father orders before directing one of the men to raise Sky's jaw. "I want to see him."

"If you so much as touch him—" I gasp out the words. "I swear to God, I will feed you to my shark."

My father rubs his jaw, clearly intrigued. "All this time, believing you were just a stubborn colt that just needed the right man to tame her."

"If you so much as touch him, I swear to God, I will feed you to my shark." I can't come up with more than the same repetitive words. It's taking too much effort to stay awake.

"All this time selecting suitors with care—" he goes on, unhindered by my words, "Screening endless ones, trying to find the right one, and you've been hiding him the whole time. Seems we both have secrets."

I claw at the bedsheets, adrenaline waging a war against the chemicals assaulting my body. "If you so much as touch him—"

He holds up a hand before squatting to scrutinize Sky, tilting his head, tilting it more, Force's smile an infection that plagues his face. All the muscles in Sky's neck tense with need, craving to harm the man who has tortured my family. Who has tortured me. Sky's jaw is harder than diamonds in the rough. His eyes like the earth ready to crack open and swallow my father whole.

Force narrows his eyes, matching Sky's before he slaps his legs and rises. "Well, I suppose there's only one thing to do with him…"

"Force, I—" I get ready to repeat my statement, reiterate it, but my father interjects.

"Invite him to dinner."

I pass out.

To be continued……

The Temple

Discussion Questions

1. Discuss or write about Bliss's words, "There is no way to soften the blow." Bliss lives in the Temple with the most advanced technology and amenities and yet, this statement is revealing. Was abuse for slaves any less painful because their masters still fed and sheltered them? Does Bliss suffer less because of her environment? Consider this in regard to "high-class" prostitution. Is it the environment or the acts done that matter?

2. Consider Bliss's reflecting on Temple recruiters and if they told the truth in their ads about the requirements needed for Temple girls. Does it sound like a trade one should encourage? Does it sound like something a woman or girl would ever want to apply for?

3. During the second interaction with Bliss, Force records the event and sends the feeds to Drake. In our time, this is defined as child pornography, though the legal age has been lowered in Bliss's time. Research the facts about and the deeds done in pornography. National Center on Sexual Exploitation and Fight the New Drug are good starts.

4. During this interaction: Bliss smiles. Even as Serenity whips her, Bliss smiles. Does this happen in pornography? Discuss what might be happening *behind* the screen and how what's on screen is a manipulation. However one "acts", does it change what is being done and make it acceptable? How are children affected by the portrayal

of pornography?

5. Bliss says she doesn't want to be rescued and can't be saved. Research the mindset of those in sex-trafficking. In light of this, discuss the negatives of "rescue" work and "hero" mindsets and how these are not helpful and can be damaging to those in sex-trafficking. (Disclaimer: this discussion relates to adult women and *not* children)

6. Luc ponders his father's words and how they influenced him. And how the world told him the same. Discuss how young boys can be shaped by the messages around them. What sort of messages does the culture send to boys? What about other environments? Are there similarities?

7. 65-95% of those in prostitution were sexually assaulted as children. This is true for Bliss. In light of this combined with deception, is Bliss's mindset more understandable, including her desire to live and die in the Temple? What can it teach us about reaching women in those environments? i.e choosing to see the little girl inside?

Resources

RACHEL MORAN: PAID FOR: MY JOURNEY THROUGH PROSTITU-
TION: https://www.amazon.com/dp/B00C7735X8

EXODUS CRY'S DOCUMENTARIES: NEFARIOUS: MERCHANT OF SOULS
AND LIBERATED: THE NEW SEXUAL REVOLUTION
(AVAILABLE ON NETFLIX):
https://exoduscry.com/tag/documentary/

A CALL TO MEN:
http://www.acalltomen.org/about-us/our-leadership

NITA BELLES: IN OUR BACKYARD:
http://inourbackyard.org/media-publications/

NATIONAL CENTER ON SEXUAL EXPLOITATION:
https://endsexualexploitation.org/videos/

REBECCA BENDER:
https://rebeccabender.org/

WOMEN AT RISK, INTERNATIONAL:
https://warinternational.org/

FOR MINNESOTA:

TRAFFICKING JUSTICE:
https://traffickingjustice.com/

REBECCA KOTZ:
http://www.rebeccakotz.com/

BREAKING FREE:
http://www.breakingfree.net/

JOHN TURNIPSEED:
https://johnturnipseed.com/,
https://urbanventures.org/—(good coffee)

DON'T BUY IT PROJECT:
https://www.dontbuyitproject.org/

Acknowledgements

As ALWAYS, I SAY A big thank you to my husband for being ready to listen to me read my books to him and to bounce off ideas or brainstorm out loud. You're my sounding board and my sticky note board all in one.

To Francine Rivers for *Redeeming Love* because it inspired me to tackle Bliss's voice when before, this book would have only been from Serenity's viewpoint.

NANO: This book and its second part was one big blur in NANO month. All 130k plus. And I'm still not sure how I managed to write that many words in one month, but NANO gave me the deadline and the pressure.

A special thank you to my oldest daughter for taking long naps so I could have time to write The Temple and The Temple Twins in the month of November.

To the CTP Team: you've gone through some major trials and you're still fighting and still working. A big thank you to my editor for getting this edited so fast, especially when I've been so delayed in getting the edits back on time! Sorry not sorry for the cliffhanger.

To all the anti-trafficking organizations out there in the trenches doing intervention, rescue work, awareness, prevention etc. Especially to Exodus Cry for my training, which helped shape the discussion questions for this book. And to Rachel Moran and her incredible work, Paid For, which helped Bliss evolve and also gave new light to the discussion questions.

To my street team, old and new members alike. You are so valuable! Please keep reading because I depend so much on you!

To my Savior for strengthening me on this journey and giving me the drive to stick with it. I'm so glad I didn't stop writing.

About the
Author

EMILY SHORE IS A MN author with a B.A. in Creative Writing from Metro State University and was a grand prize winner of #PitchtoPublication, which led her to working with professionals in the publishing industry. Her anti-trafficking books Ruby in the Rough and Ruby in the Ruins are her first indie-published books with proceeds benefiting trafficking rescue organizations. She is signed with Clean Teen Publishing for her anti-trafficking dystopian The Aviary. For every book sold, a personal donation will return to Women At Risk, International.

Throughout the years, she has connected with rescue organizations and survivors of sex-trafficking and injects the truths she's learned into her books for youth. She loves motivational speaking on the issue of sex-trafficking and always hopes for more speaking events in schools, churches, and libraries. Please contact her on her website if you are interested in hearing her speak. In her spare time, she loves attending any abolition events, baking, acrylic painting, interior decorating, and spending time with all the little girls in her life.

Emily lives in Saint Paul with her husband and two daughters. Their goal is to adopt a little girl from India.